THE LAST ENEMY

Book Three of
the Last Enemy Series

dan e. hendrickson

Dedication

This one is for my wonderful wife, Cheryl.
The last Enemy is about family and friends
sticking together and being there for one another.
Cheryl you are my partner, my wife, my family.
Like Jim said about Linda in the book, "Every
success I've known in life has been with her."
That's the way I feel about you, honey.

Thank You

First, I am grateful to God for all that great things
He has given me, and how His love inspires me to
be the best I can be. Then I am thankful for all the
wonderful people who helped me to put together
this series. Susie Catlin for her amazing original
water color portraits. Rebeccah Hendrickson,
my daughter, for her help with editing and
proofreading. Teresa Jackson for her wonderful
editing contributions, and for David Navarro my
chief editor. The Last Enemy series has been a real
ride and a great journey.
Thanks for taking it with me.

Contents

Chapter One

Abduction

Maximillian Manerez, the most powerful cartel leader in Mexico and Central America, controls ninety percent of the drug trafficking for the Eastern United States, and has begun to take over the Western half as well. Although he would never admit it to anyone, much of his recent success has been due to that annoying daughter of former Mexican Presidente Tomar Gonzalez, Marnia, The Cartel Crusher.

Her passion to take down Anthony Santiago's human trafficking and slavery cartel in Central Mexico is the single biggest reason he is the most powerful among the remaining cartels. He knows that it is just a matter of time before she begins to turn her annoying vendetta on him and his operations. He has no faith in his son, Jonathan, being able to manipulate Marnia for very long and fears that their relationship could turn against him before either he or his son can stop the catastrophic consequences that would involve.

He tried to explain to Boris that he had no time to dedicate the massive resources it would take to successfully sabotage an American plane so that he could kill the Edwards family. Boris would not listen and made it clear that either Maximillian would handle the job or Boris would move his own business interests to other clients. Max knew he needed Boris's support and services in order to remain the number one cartel.

Boris was not someone who could be threatened. Whenever one of Maximillian's associates got that stupid, he ended up sending flowers to their widows. No, this ex-assassin held cards that even Maximillian could not overlook. So he put his cat-and-mouse game with Marnia Gonzalez on hold to do what Boris wanted. After weeks of planning and work, everything was in place, and all the right people were paid off at the Los Angeles International Airport.

Max never liked how much power Boris held over him. After doing some subtle investigating of his own, he finally understood why Edwards Auto was so vital to Boris's operation. Once he figured that out he knew exactly what to do to gain future leverage over Boris.

Getting the airport security people to ignore the maintenance crews hiding the explosive charges was very expensive, but Boris had deep pockets and every time Maximillian asked for more funds, they were immediately made available. Much to his amusement, Max had Boris unwittingly funding his surreptitious plan to gain leverage over Boris. The irony of that brought Max great pleasure.

Max was not stupid, though. He knew Boris's people would be watching, so the timing had to be perfect to keep the Edwards family from boarding while making it appear like they did.

Los Angeles International Airport

Jacob loved flying. His wife, Mary, and mother Linda, however, barely tolerated the ordeal. When they landed in L.A. at 11:00 a.m. Pacific Time, both women needed to take a long walk and drink lots of water, which worked out just fine because the next flight was on the other side of the airport. Jacob did not mind carrying his mother's carryon luggage to the next gate, and Mary considered it good exercise to carry her own.

The three of them were a little disappointed that Jacob's father, Jim, decided not to go with them, but they were not surprised. In fact, Linda made the comment that at one point she thought it was just going to be her and Mary—so she was absolutely thrilled that Jacob decided to go.

Jacob and Mary did not tell Linda about Mary's condition. They decided to wait until they got to Australia where they had an appointment with a specialist. Mary did not want to worry Linda about any potential troubles on the long flight, even though her symptoms, like morning sickness and cramps, were practically nonexistent.

When Danielle was born, Mary's doctor told her that having another child was too dangerous but Mary's mother Isabella was a maternity nurse in South Texas and kept her ears open for any advancements in medical science that would allow her daughter to try again to have another child. She gave them information about a new treatment that allowed women like Mary to have a much more stable pregnancy and delivery.

One of the most experienced doctors in the world using this treatment operated out of Australia. The trip to Australia suggested by Linda was a perfect excuse to go and see this doctor personally. The medication prescribed for this treatment had already stabilized her body to the point that she was almost one hundred percent functional, unlike twenty-two years ago when she was nineteen and pregnant with Danielle after having married Jacob right after her eighteenth birthday.

Linda Edwards loved spending time with her son and his wife more than anything in the whole world. She never fully wrapped her head around what happened in Cozumel ten years ago, but she was just thankful that it brought her only child home again. To Linda, the "grownups" in the Edwards' household were her, Mary, and Danielle—and taking care of "the boys" was a full-time job that they all happily shared. She was thrilled to get on that plane to go see someplace she had never seen before, and even more ecstatic that she would get to enjoy it with her children. With all the reminiscing done, Linda smiles and knows it's now time to board the next plane.

Jacob points out that their plane is already boarding as they round a corner in the terminal. Joining the line, Jacob hears their names called to please go to the desk. A short Mexican-American gentleman tells them that there is a problem with their tickets and says it will take a few minutes to straighten out. The girls, flabbergasted, begin to ask why and what's the problem, but Jacob's nineteen years in the military has exposed him to plenty of paperwork errors and red tape and he tells his wife and mom to sit down so he can handle it.

They begrudgingly sit behind him as Jacob turns to the short man and says, "What is the problem actually?" The man stares at his computer screen scrolling up and down looking for something.

"We somehow lost your seat assignments," he says, "and I am trying to locate three seats in a row for you in coach, but I'm coming up with nothing."

Jacob rolls his eyes knowing that there is no way his mother would ever settle for anything less than all three sitting together. The man behind the counter looks over at the line of people boarding, then back at his screen, then back at the line. Jacob asks him if he should be concerned about missing the flight once the plane is fully boarded. The man assures him that the plane will not take off until this situation is resolved. After some more fidgeting on his screen, all the passengers have boarded the plane except the Edwards trio. Jacob feels the laser beam stares of his mother and Mary.

"Look buddy," Jacob says as he glares at the man, "we need to figure this out right now."

The man's phone rings and he answers a couple of questions in Spanish, then looks at Jacob, "You can board now. We have put your whole family in first class. We apologize for the wait."

Jacob gives a big old smile. "Well that is more like it."

Linda bolts for the desk when she hears the news to make sure she will not be charged for the upgrade. The man assures her that no extra charges were added to her credit card. He prints the new tickets and hands them to her. The three dash into the boarding ramp tunnel connected to the transcontinental aircraft that waits for them at the far end. Three quarters of the way to the airplane a side door opens and a big man in a security uniform steps in and halts the trio with his flashlight.

"Stand to the side," he says motioning, "we need to evacuate three sick passengers. This will only take a minute, sorry for any inconvenience."

"Is it something contagious?" Mary asks.

"Nah, just some kind of food poisoning from some restaurant meal they had at the last airport they were at."

Three men emerge from around the corner, each pushing wheel chairs, a Caucasian man and older woman and a Latino woman. Jacob is struck by their similarity to his own trio and alarmed that they are even dressed almost exactly the same.

Jacob casts a quick glance at the big security guy then instantly whirls around to the girls and yells, "Run!"

But it's too late, before Jacob can even start to run the security man shoves his flashlight into Jacob's face and blows a vapor from an attached nozzle into his mouth and nostrils that drops him instantly. Two others grab Linda and Mary and give them the same treatment. The three in the wheel chairs get up, step around the Edwards trio, unconscious on the floor, and grab their luggage and belongings, then board the plane.

The security man and wheel chair pushers whisk the unconscious trio down a side flight of stairs to the tarmac. They put them in a transport and take them out to a waiting ambulance. The ambulance transports them to a dock where they are put in a cargo container and loaded onto a ship belonging to Maximillian to be transported to one of his compounds in Central America.

* * *

Jacob awakens two days later in what looks like a hospital room. He springs to a seated position and discovers his wife Mary and mother Linda in similar beds. All are handcuffed to their beds. He shakes his head trying to clear the grogginess and make sense of his predicament when two Latino men walk into the room. One is an older, very elaborately dressed man smoking an expensive Cuban cigar, and the other is some type of medical doctor.

"Well Mr. Edwards, how nice of you to join the land of the living," says the well-dressed man as he drags on his cigar. "My name is Maximillian Manerez. I am sure you have many questions, but let me start by saying that it is the greatest of honors to have the Hero of Cozumel grace my home."

Jacob remembers hearing this man's name somewhere. It seems there was some kind of drug lord who funded pirates down in Central America who went by that name when he was on active duty. Jacob's wife and mother begin to stir and awaken.

"So," Jacob says, "is this some kind of kidnapping for ransom. I'm sure my father will meet your demands. What are your terms?"

Maximillian chuckles. "Oh Commander, this is a kidnapping all right," he nods his head and the ashes drop off the tip of his cigar, "but your father could not even come close to paying me what you are worth."

"What do you mean?" Jacob says as he yanks lightly at his cuffs and casts a concerned look at his stirring wife and mother. "Why kidnap us then, what is going on?"

"Please Jacob," Max says putting his hand up, palm toward Jacob, "call me Max, and do not fear, your lovely wife, unborn child, and mother are perfectly safe at this time."

Jacob, visibly shaken, tries to sit up even more but is hindered by the restraints. "How do you know my wife is pregnant?"

Max, a little intimidated, steps back. He knows this prisoner is no one to trifle with. However, the restraints are doing the job and he quickly regains his composure.

"Dr. Chavez had to take blood samples from all of you when you arrived to be sure that the anesthetics we used did not have any harmful effects. That is when we found out that your wife is pregnant."

Mary and Linda, fully awake, are taking the conversation in and are obviously distressed. Jacob casts a reassuring glance at them. "Before we proceed," Max interrupts the moment, "I would like the three of you to look at the TV monitor over here. I want you to understand what is going on."

They all look as Dr. Chavez tunes in an American television station broadcasting the news that the plane they supposedly boarded in L.A. crash-landed in the Pacific Ocean. Max looks at each of them with feigned compassion. "To the outside world, you three are dead. The only ones who know your true identities and that you are alive are me, my son Jonathan, and Dr. Chavez. Everyone else has been…shall we say…disposed."

Simultaneously Mary and Linda cry out and scream hysterically, but Max is ready. Dr. Chavez gives them a mild tranquilizer to calm them and asks Jacob if he needs the same.

Jacob composes himself. "That won't be necessary. But since you have successfully pulled off this stunt, why don't you explain to me what the hell is going on then?"

Max sees no harm in letting them in on the details, so he begins to unfold a story that has been twenty years in the making.

After nineteen years in the Coast Guard and six years of commanding a ship of the line, Jacob is not one to be shocked or surprised by anything he hears or sees, but the story Max tells is almost beyond comprehension and blows his mind.

With furrowed brows, Jacob shakes his head slightly and says, "So you're saying that the wrinkled old annoying Russian dealer from New York has been gunning for me and my family since before Cozumel, and he set this whole plane crash thing up?" He pauses, then adds, "He holds so much power over men like you that you kidnapped us to use as leverage against him someday?"

Max takes a long drag on his cigar. "That wrinkled, old Russian is a world class assassin known as The Chameleon. He's one of the most successful in modern history. He retired from hire in the late eighties and started building money laundering operations all over the world. By the time he got to South America he was one of the most powerful underworld bosses in Europe and Asia and therefore pretty much untouchable by any of my associates. But, he did not come in to take over our operations, rather to broker our finances. You see, making money in the United States is easy; getting it out is very difficult and expensive. Boris devised a network by which he smuggles our money over the border in his auctioned wholesale cars. Once we get the vehicles out of the United States, retrieving our money is quite easy. Boris charges us fifteen percent off the top. Most conventional money laundering can cost four times that amount. So, you can imagine how popular and powerful a man like that could become in my world."

Jacob immediately thinks back to that time in his office with Chuck Yeager talking about a "Russian James Bond." He can hardly believe it. He looks down into his lap shaking his head. "That fucking Russian James Bond was right there in front of my face all that time and I could not see it." In the moment of silence that follows, Jacob realizes something that makes him irate in a very calm and cold way. "So that means that Dad and Danielle are in big trouble as well, doesn't it?"

Jacob's intensity unsettles Max and he instinctively steps back away from this very dangerous man before him, forgetting for a moment that he is well secured to the bed. He quietly orders some of his armed men to come into the infirmary and keep Jacob under control.

Max sternly bores his eyes into Jacob's. "Never forget, Commander, you are in my house. Although I have my own reasons, I did save your lives in the process. Boris is not in a position to move against your father and Danielle at this time. With him thinking you all are dead, he will once again endeavor to purchase Edwards Auto from your family."

"And if he does, we will be worthless to you. Huh, Max?"

Max laughs loudly. "On the contrary, Jacob, you see, you and your mother are on the board of trustees for the corporation. Your father could never sell it without all of your signatures. Even if Boris gets Jim to sell, I would merely have to let Boris know that you are all still alive and in my custody. The mere threat of revealing you are alive would give me great influence over him."

"Where does that leave us then? Are we just going to wait around until Boris makes a move one way or another? Are we just supposed to sit on our thumbs here in your private little hacienda and do nothing while my little girl and my dad think we are dead?"

Max is truly amused and tells Jacob that he is not necessarily where he thinks he may be. The facility that Maximillian has Jacob, his wife, and his mother in is a privately owned maximum security prison. He refuses to tell Jacob what country they are in, but lets him know that as the owner of the prison, he is one hundred percent in control.

Dr. Chavez informs Jacob that he is aware of Mary's peculiar condition involving her pregnancy and has already contacted a very good OBGYN doctor who is very familiar with the treatments she is receiving. He assures him that as long as she is in his care, she will receive the very best that medical science has to offer.

"You see," says Max, "The more heirs there are to Edwards Auto, the more profitable it will be to me, and the more motivated I am to protect all of you. So that's good for you, no?"

Before Jacob can respond, Linda says, "We will not give you any problems at all if you will guarantee that my daughter-in-law will have the very best care and that we will be allowed to take care of the baby ourselves."

She then looks at her son and says, "When were you going to tell me, Jacob?"

Jacob clears his throat. "We had an appointment in Australia with the world's leading expert for Mary's condition and once we landed, we were going to tell you everything, Mom."

Linda, groggy from the tranquilizer, seems to almost be drifting off to sleep when she says, "Jacob, I forbid you from making any aggressive moves against Mr. Max so he can guarantee that Mary will receive the best treatment and have a healthy baby."

Max assures them that he will absolutely take care of them as Linda succumbs to sleep.

Chapter Two

Prison Life

Manerez Private Prison, Three Months Later

Max stares out his office window thinking on his present situation. He should have guessed that mixing Jacob with a bunch of low life criminals was a bad idea. At first, he insisted that the Edwards trio stay in the little cottage he set up for them, but Jacob went stir crazy and begged to at least use the workout facility. After Jonathan spoke up for Jacob, Max grudgingly agreed to let him, but gave him a fake name and prisoner's garb so he could blend in, and made him grow a beard and mustache to help conceal his identity to the rest of the prison population. He also made sure that all the guards knew to keep a very close eye on Jacob and keep him out of trouble. Max shakes his head and walks away from his window to pour himself some tequila.

Jacob is glad Max has allowed him the liberty to use the workout area and wants to go a few rounds on a punching bag. He strolls out into the workout yard seeking a heavy bag. Several others are in the boxing section working the punching bags and Jacob heads over to join them. The Latinos welcome Jacob with eager anticipation at having a little fun with the new gringo— until they see Jacob work the bag. At forty-nine years old, Jacob has moves that put the twenty-year-olds to shame with things they can't do, and his power is something to behold. After a full twenty minutes of nonstop aggression, Jacob saunters over to the benches to take a break.

"Were you a pro?" one of the guys asks as Jacob slugs down some water.

Jacob, glad someone speaks English, responds "No. I did a lot of kickboxing when I was in high school in the states, but never really had a chance to go pro. I joined the military, got married, you know." Jacob knows some Spanish, being married to Mary for almost twenty three years, but finds it difficult to carry on a lengthy conversation in the language.

"So how did you end up here in Max's prison? No one recognizes you. This place is usually for his people who get caught, or are being punished by Max, or are taking the hit as a fall guy for some scheme?"

Having been specifically briefed by Max and his son Jonathan on how to answer this question, Jacob says, "I got in a little financial trouble in the states, so, I came down here to make a quick buck smuggling and lost a whole shipment of Max's Cuban cigars at sea. He put me here to teach me a lesson."

A big heavyweight working one of the bags stops and looks at Jacob with a devilish grin. "So, you're the one that did the night run to the island for Max and lost that shipment, huh? You're lucky Max didn't cut off your hand for that one hombre."

Jacob nods. "Yes, aren't we all subject to Max's mercy around here."

The big guy laughs as he removes his gloves and steps over in front of Jacob. Two of his friends join them.

The big guy says, "You know, when I did that run I would always get home late, hombre."

"Oh yeah, why's that?" The hairs on the back of Jacob's neck start to stand up.

"Amigo, at that hour of the evening in that port, there are plenty of little niñas ripe for the taking, and me and my hombres here would always help ourselves."

Despite Cozumel, Jacob did not consider himself a violent man, but he did have his limits, and the sexual exploitation of children was one of them. Immediately Jacob sizes up the large Latino man before him, six foot two inches, two hundred twenty pounds of strong, lean muscle, but he stands a little cockeyed on his right foot and his left shoulder droops a bit. The guy has obvious injuries, and that spells weaknesses. Jacob compares to the man at the same height, two hundred ten pounds, and as demonstrated earlier, is in exquisite condition for a man his age. He stands up and places himself in the most strategic position among the trio. "So, you like to rape little girls, do you?"

The man sneers and pushes Jacob back. "You got a problem with me, gringo?"

Jacob knows that he has already crossed a line with this guy so he simply taunts the man further, "Cabrón."

The large Latino screams as he cocks back and throws a powerful right cross at Jacob's face. Jacob anticipates the move, fades to the right, blocking the cross with his left hand, catching and holding it while simultaneously smashing the man's left shoulder with his own right straight vertical punch. He instep kicks the man's left knee with his right foot. The big man screams in agony as his left side collapses. Jacob finishes him off with a right karate chop just below his left ear above the jaw, knocking him out immediately.

The Latino's two friends try to grab Jacob, but he front kicks the one to his right straight in the groin dropping him immediately, and head butts the other one to the left breaking his nose and dropping him to the ground as well.

With all three on the ground, Jacob is still not done. He jumps on the unconscious big one and starts to pummel him in the face with his fists. "So, you like to rape little girls? You piece of shit." He starts kneeing him in the groin several times until finally the guards, who were way too slow at responding in the first place, drag him off the half dead pedophile he was punishing.

A few hours later, Jacob is cooling off in a private lockup cell. It is no mystery to him that child rapists bring out the killer in him. Ever since that yacht murder and child rape incident off of Honduras in '96, he knew he crossed that line. His dad always used to say there is a difference between being capable of hurting or killing, and actually wanting to do it. Jacob had talked to many combat veterans over the years and they understood. For them, it was a matter of self-preservation, or protecting their buddies in combat. You do what you have to do to stay alive and get the job done. If that means killing the enemy, then so be it. But then, there are those who come out of a traumatic experience, a betrayal, or a horrific situation where something snaps in the individual and won't let them tolerate that kind of thing again. They will punish those who try, oftentimes to an extreme. That's what happened to him on that yacht when that thirteen-year-old girl died in his arms.

That's also why he pushed Danielle to be able to defend herself. Mary would get so mad at him for pushing her to be an expert fighter. "What do you want, a world champion MMA fighter for a daughter?" she would say when they would come in from a two-hour workout.

Jacob's response was always the same, "No, but my daughter will never be a victim. No one will ever lay a hand on her without her permission." Mary knew Jacob's motivation and she tolerated the training only because she saw that Danielle enjoyed it. The bonding between father and daughter was also good. After Cozumel, he really tried to keep himself out of situations where he would have to deal with the kind of vermin that did horrible things to children.

He hears a rap at the door and Max's son, Jonathan, shouts from the other side, "If I come in, are you going to force me to have my men shoot you?"

He can't believe he's gotten friendly with this guy while being his father's prisoner. But somehow, a weird bond, almost even buddy status, has evolved between them over the last couple months. "No, come in. You won't have to shoot me Jonathan."

The son of Maximillian Manerez, head of the biggest crime cartel in Mexico and Central America, steps in with a couple of Gallo lagers in his hands and tosses one to Jacob. He opens his and sits down on the cot next to him, "My God, Jacob, Dr. Chavez doesn't think he can fix Frankie's testicles. You may have just turned him into a eunuch!"

Despite himself, Jacob coughs up his swig of beer as he laughs at Jonathan's comment. "I'm sorry, Jonathan, but how could I guess that somebody was going to come over and start bragging about raping kids."

Jonathan gives a big huff of air. "Jacob, this is a prison. We have murderers, thieves, bank robbers, and yes, child molesters in here. In fact, I put Frankie in here for that reason. My dad and I are bad men, and we have made a fortune doing very bad things, but what Frankie does to kids is something neither of us will ever tolerate. I probably will kill that slime ball myself someday."

Jacob takes another swig of beer and almost loses that mouthful as he chokes out the words, "Well, maybe you won't have to now that Frankie is going to be an 'it' for the rest of his life." They both laugh so hard that they spill some of their beers on the floor. After settling down, Jonathan invites Jacob to head back out to his cottage with him. Jacob and Jonathan pass by a huge lot of at least a thousand cars of all makes and models, as they walk through the compound. Jacob recognizes that most of them have a Manheim Auto Auction run number sticker on the windshield. "So those are the cars that Boris sends your money in?"

Jonathan raises his eyebrows as he glances over and says, "Yes, and I am running out of room for the damn things. Sooner or later I'm going to have to figure out what to do with them."

"Why don't you sell them? I know that what they are worth is nothing compared to the money they bring in them, but they are still cars and worth some money. You are a businessman; I can't help but think that wasting them would drive you out of your mind."

Jonathan raises both hands in a helpless gesture. "Well I would love to sell them to anyone, but they get all torn up when we retrieve the money from them, and frankly I cannot justify the cost of putting them back together down here. I certainly cannot pay to ship them back to the states to have it done."

Jacob is his father's son, and the old Edwards Auto mental wheels start turning in his head at about a mile a second. "Well, Jonathan I am about the best automotive reconditioning guy on the east coast, next to my old man, and I need something to do. You have a whole compound here full of free labor. I can manage a crew to get these units retail ready. You can recoup some of your money from having to buy them, and I can have something to do that will keep me out of trouble. What do you say?"

Jonathan stops right in the middle of the yard looks at Jacob. "Wow, that is a truly fantastic idea. I am going to get my guards to organize some work crews to help you. We have an old army carpool facility adjacent to the prison that we can set up for that."

As they continue walking Jacob turns and looks Jonathan sternly in the eye. "I swear to God, Jonathan, you put one rapist pedophile in any of those crews, and you'll find them the next day cut in pieces and decomposing in a wheel acid barrel."

Jonathan stops, studies him for a second. "What is a wheel acid barrel?" They both just start laughing all over again as they continue the rest of the way back to his home where Mary and Linda are waiting.

Compared to the rest of the prison, the cottage they have been living in for several months is quite luxurious. Jonathan tells them about Jacob's new job, but conveniently leaves out the fight earlier that day in the exercise yard. Before he leaves, Jonathan looks at everyone and says, "I told you all I would keep you updated on Jim and Danielle's status. Apparently, Danielle is moving down to South Texas to live with Mary's mother and father. My sources tell me that she tried to get Jim to go with her, but he refused. Jim has recently made Danielle a trustee to the company, so anything that happens to Edwards Auto now lies in her hands as well. I believe she is going to Roberto and Isabella's for emotional reasons and that she does intend to return someday to help Jim. I hope this news is not too disturbing to you."

He thanks Jonathan for the update and tells him they will talk it over in private. Jonathan bids them farewell and Jacob looks at his wife, Mary, now in her sixth month of pregnancy. She is obviously very happy about the situation with Danielle. Much to his surprise, so is his mother. Linda says that it is good that they are separated right now so Boris has a harder time keeping tabs on the both of them. Mary adds that her parents will protect Danielle in ways that none of them can imagine, and that this is God's hand working in the situation. Jacob can't help but agree.

He does not say anything out loud because he is sure that his apartment is bugged. But with his new job, he thinks he just figured out a way to let the outside world know they are alive, and possibly get the attention of a newly promoted captain of the Mexican Military's Anti-Cartel Task Force.

Present Day, Office of Deputy Director Chuck Yeager of the Philadelphia FBI

Deputy Director Chuck Yeager sits in his office with Captain Marnia Gonzalez of the Mexican Anti-Cartel Task Force discussing the details of the infamous case regarding the luxury yacht incident off South Padre Island near Coast Guard Station Brazos one month earlier. The bosses of a money laundering crime syndicate planned a forced marriage of Danielle Edwards to Yuri Sebastion. The crime syndicate's U.S. holdings are in Yuri's name, so by forcing the marriage and killing Jim Edwards, owner of Edwards Auto, and his granddaughter and heir, Danielle, they attempted to steal Edwards Auto, where they had established a money laundering scheme using auctioned autos to smuggle money into Mexico and Central America.

As they sort through the details, they both agree that certain decades-old major cases they each are working on are connected to one individual man, Boris Rasmov. The crime lord has remained almost completely transparent to any crime-fighting organization in the world until one month ago when his cover was miraculously blown and he was captured by Marnia. She responded to and helped in the rescue effort of the Edwards where she nabbed Boris and then took him back to Mexico to be prosecuted for—among other things—the murder of Commander Jacob Edwards of the United States Coast Guard; his wife, Mary; and his mother, Linda by way of a plane crash that he orchestrated three years ago.

They also discuss how thirteen years ago, Commander Jacob Edwards rescued Captain Marnia as a young girl of eighteen from being raped and murdered by the notorious pirate and cage-fighting champion, Dominik Thrace, on a cruise ship twenty nautical miles off its port of departure in Cozumel, Mexico.

People all over Central America and the Caribbean who knew the pirate's fearsome reputation were completely flabbergasted that Commander Edwards defeated such an animal in hand-to-hand combat. They were astounded even more that not only did Jacob defeat the vile pirate, but after rendering him broken and unconscious he also took him up to the highest platform on the cruise ship and flung him to his death. From that day forward, Jacob was known in Central American and Caribbean circles as the Hero of Cozumel.

Chuck tells Marnia that he is not the least surprised that his friend, Jacob Edwards, so easily defeated such a monster. Jacob was an extraordinarily gifted martial arts and combat expert. He relates to Marnia how he and Jacob boarded a yacht off the coast of Honduras back in '96 before Cozumel. They discovered a Mexican finance minister and his family brutally murdered in the main cabin, and one of his children, a thirteen-year-old girl, raped and severely beaten. Jacob tried to help but the girl died in his arms. The impact of that incident dramatically changed the young lieutenant. His rage for individuals who torment and abuse women and children almost cost him his Coast Guard career early on; but Chuck, his best friend, Mary, his wife, and having a newborn daughter, Danielle, helped him deal with and get control of his rage.

Jacob went on to become one of the most dynamic officers in the Coast Guard. His prowess as a leader and tactician earned him different commands. Because of his command exploits in the Coast Guard he was affectionately called by his men The Commander and came to be known by that title to all in the Coast Guard who heard of him. His heroic act on the cruise ship off the coast of Cozumel cost him his military career, though, because he executed a man at sea. But he was glad to return to Pennsylvania with his family to help his father, Jim Edwards, run the family auto wholesaling business in Manheim.

Chuck and Marnia continue to discuss how the Edwards were not aware that Boris Rasmov, the notorious crime lord and ex-assassin, had targeted Edwards Auto in Manheim as the business he wanted to control to use for his money smuggling operations. Boris set up the Cozumel incident to lure Jacob to respond to the duress call simply so he could assassinate him, thus eliminating a principal heir to the Edwards' business. When that plan failed, it took Boris almost ten years to infiltrate Edwards Auto as a wholesale client and later a tenant of the business property. The Edwards were unaware when they rented a building at Edwards Auto to a Russian man who used the facility to prepare cars for auction, that they had rented it to this notorious crime lord and ex-assassin who used the facility to prepare cars to smuggle money out of the U.S.

Boris used the trucking end of the business to cleverly transport his vehicles filled with concealed money to the Mexican border, where he could securely transfer the money to his true clients, the drug and human trafficking cartels. He tried again and again to buy Edwards Auto from the Edwards, making lucrative offers, but Jim refused. Since they would not sell, he targeted the family for extermination and devised a plan to kill most of the family in a plane crash while they were en route to Australia for a vacation. Jim and Danielle refused to go on vacation for various reasons, so the plan only succeeded in part, eliminating three of the five Edwards.

Boris despised spending another three years to plan and prepare to successfully eliminate the final two members of the Edwards family and legally gain control of the company. That's where the whole ruse of the dance school recruiting and *The Royal Princess II* came into play. They tricked Danielle into signing a marriage license with his nephew, Yuri Sebastion, by pretending they were auction documents. Then they used the excuse of dance company recruitment to get them all to board *The Royal*

Princess II cruise ship at Station Brazos to kill them all at sea in a feigned pirate attack.

The plan almost worked but through a series of events that Chuck and Marnia agree can only be labeled as a miracle of God, Boris's whole plan blew up in his face on that cruise ship resulting in his defeat and capture by U.S. and Mexican forces. To prevent his nephew, Yuri, from spilling his guts to authorities, Boris killed him with a harpoon gun in Mexican controlled waters, allowing Marnia to arrest Boris and take him back to her country for prosecution.

Marnia explains to Chuck that Boris was an integral part of the cartel activity going on in her country for decades. While she was taking down the cartels, especially the Santiago Cartel, her allies, like Rosemary Sargent, the Mexico City brothel owner, and Jonathan Manerez, the son of the boss of the Manerez Cartel, the other largest cartel in the region, refused to talk about a certain elusive and terrifying man behind all the operations. She now knows this man is Boris, The Chameleon, as he is called. Anyone who crosses Boris simply disappears. With his secretive ability to find and deal death to his enemies, he instills a stone-cold fear and silence in almost anyone who knows him. When she arrested her own great uncle, Pedro Guerra, for human trafficking and his deep connections to the Santiago Cartel, he was gunned down by a sniper as she escorted him to the prison transport. There on the steps of his building, in his dying breath, even he only spoke the name Boris, but nothing else.

Chuck tells Marnia that when she took down Anthony Santiago three years ago in the battle at the western half of Falcon Lake, it was one of the most fantastic things he had ever heard. Most law enforcement agencies in the U.S. are very aware of and quite enamored with the reputation of The Cartel Crusher, the daughter of an ex-president of Mexico who grew up and defied all odds to succeed where most had miserably failed. She eliminated six cartels in less than two years, a feat unheard of in Mexican law enforcement. Marnia reiterates to Chuck that the aid of so many good men and women, like Rosemary Sargent and Jonathan Manerez, were the key to her success.

"Marnia," Chuck says staring her square in the eyes, "if what we believe is true and Danielle's family is still alive, then Jonathan has been keeping it from you for three years now. If he is truly an ally, then his excuse has to be beyond fantastic, to say the least."

Marnia's eyes penetrate Chuck with an intensity he's never seen. She stands, hands on hips, and says, "Chuck, I'm not going to lie to you. I'm in love with Jonathan, and until I know beyond a shadow of a doubt that he has manipulated and maliciously lied to me, I am going to hold on to the hope that he had a very good reason. Besides, Boris is the key to all of this, and if people as powerful as my uncle and Santiago were afraid of him, Jonathan could have a very good reason for his silence. But we will know soon enough, won't we?"

Chuck stands and grabs his things to leave, then turns and says, "Let's go talk to Danielle and Jim. Captain Williams has already gotten clearance for the special op from Vice President Rogers and we will sort all this stuff out as we get through this. One thing is for sure—there are a hell of a lot of unanswered questions here and it's about time they get answered."

"Agreed," Marnia says grabbing her stuff as they head out to drive from the Philadelphia FBI office to Manheim, Pennsylvania, to break some fantastic news to Danielle and Jim Edwards.

Later that Day, Manheim, Edwards Auto

Danielle is still getting used to sitting at her daddy's desk. She refuses to change anything about the office. It brings back positive and wonderful memories of her mom and dad. Grandpa Jim is out in the detail shop helping with final inspection and she is finishing up on car registrations for tomorrow's sale. She is just about done when she hears a tap on the door and she yells come in.

The door opens and in walks Captain Marnia Gonzalez of the Mexican Anti-Cartel Task Force and Deputy Director Chuck Yeager of the FBI.

Danielle jumps up and exclaims, "Chuck, Marnia! What brings you guys to Manheim? Come on in, sit down, how can I help you?" Chuck is the first to speak, "Danielle, you better sit down. We have something very serious to say to you and Jim, but we thought we would tell you first and you can help us break it to Jim."

Danielle is trying to control her emotions as she asks the duo what is going on. Marnia leans forward holding Danielle's gaze and says, "Danielle, your father, your mother, and your grandmother are all still alive."

Danielle is stunned into silence as she tries to comprehend the words that just came out of Marnia's mouth. Dizzy with hysteria, she leans back and stares incredulously at the two people before her. "How can this be?" she manages to say.

Chuck Yeager responds. "Well, Danielle, that is why we did not say anything about our suspicions last month at Brazos Station. We did not really see how it could be, because by all the records from the L.A. International Airport, the three of them did board the plane. As you already know, they were bumped to first class because of some screw up with their seating arrangements. What you might not know is that just before they boarded, three people were taken off the plane, a forty-something Caucasian man, his forty-something Latina wife, and an older Caucasian woman. The record shows that they were put on an ambulance and then whisked away. Funny thing is, no one ever investigated what happened to them."

She leans forward, "So you two think that the people that got on that ambulance were my parents, and grandmother?"

"All the footage from the airport shows three unconscious people being taken through the airport, but the video feed from the airplane shows three people getting into the wheelchairs by their own power. In the tunnel between the airplane and the terminal, there is no camera footage available. There are no records anywhere in L.A. of a trio fitting their descriptions being taken to a hospital for food poisoning," Marnia adds.

Danielle leans forward and looks Marnia in the eye. "Okay, I can see how all this might lead to validating your statement earlier, but how can you be sure?"

Marnia smiles and then points to something behind Danielle. "Because of that sign on the wall behind your head, Danielle."

Danielle turns around and grabs the framed sign that Grandpa Jim had made. "How can the Coast Guard status, rank, and promotion eligibility designation of Daddy at retirement have anything to do with his being alive now?"

"Because those same symbols are on the inside panels of at least two dozen cars and trucks we have intercepted from the Manerez Cartel's new auto wholesaling business in the last year."

Marnia goes on to explain that this influx of late model vehicles into Mexico mostly through the customs office of Brownsville, Texas has piqued the interest of a lot of Mexican law enforcement for the last few years.

"Now that we know Boris was smuggling money through our country by way of those vehicles, and that the cartels were the main buyers of them, it only made sense that they would try to get rid of the vehicles somehow. We believe most cartels just junk the cars and sell them for scrap metal. But for some reason, Maximillian Manerez, the biggest of the cartel lords, went into the auto wholesaling business. In order for him to do that, he would need someone with the right skills to get these cars expertly put back together so that they would be worth something on the market.

Danielle just leans back gives a big sigh, "Daddy!"

"Yes," Marnia acknowledges, "we believe your family is being held prisoner at the Manerez private prison in Guatemala."

"Wow," Danielle says and then stares off trying to take it all in.

Marnia adds, "The cars we were able to confiscate last month in the holding yard across the border from Brownsville, Texas had almost five hundred million dollars hidden in them. We practically had to tear the cars apart to get to all the money. Some even had extra inside panels welded in to make for hidden compartments. It would be a major undertaking to make them all look normal."

Danielle huffs and blows through her closed lips before she says, "Well no one around here is better at identifying and fixing bad body work than my dad. Sometimes the condition report department at the auction will see the slightest irregularities in body work done to a collision car and flag it for frame damage. Daddy would inspect cars for those flaws and make them look factory new with our body shop work. If anyone could put those damaged smuggling cars back together and make them look normal, he could."

"What's going on here?"

Everyone immediately turns to see Jim Edwards in the doorway with a bewildered look on his face.

Danielle jumps up and over to her grandfather and asks how much of the conversation he has heard.

Jim scoots around and sits in front of Danielle's desk, "Not much, but what I did hear sounds like you're talking as if Jacob is alive."

Danielle puts a hand on her grandfather's shoulder, "Grandpa, what Chuck and Marnia are saying is that there is a very strong chance that dad, mom, and grandmother are still alive and being held prisoner in Central America."

Jim, mesmerized by the news, is all ears as they catch him up on the details. When they finish, Jim just sits there a minute in total silence, resting his chin on his palms, leaning over with his elbows to his knees. He then looks up with the biggest grin that his almost seventy-year-old face can produce, "It's a miracle, a freaking miracle! I agree with Danielle. My son is a genius when it comes to fixing and erasing any sign of frame damage or bad body work done to a vehicle. If anyone could put a car back together after Boris and his boys ruin it with retrofitted smuggling compartments, it would be him."

Marnia clears her throat with a deadpan serious look on her face as she addresses the real elephant in the room. "You all know that now that Boris is in custody, and his whole western organization is pretty much broke, Maximillian has no real motive to keep Jacob, Mary, and Linda?"

Chuck jumps in quickly. "That's very true but we cannot assume that he will try to dispose of them either. He could just let them go,"

Danielle's eyes tear up as she asks, "So where are they being held now? Are they still alive? How can you be sure they have not killed them already? It's been a month since you arrested Boris."

Marnia stands, reaches over, and puts her hand on Danielle's shoulder. "I am so sorry to put you through this merry-go-round right now. To think that you just found out your parents and grandmother are still alive, and then to tell you what danger they are in must be overwhelming. I am positive they are alive, Danielle, because the last car we got from the Manerez plant was just a few days ago. It had the same symbols on the inside left quarter panel."

"How does that prove Maximillian hasn't killed them yet?" Jim asks.

"For several reasons," Chuck adds, "but the biggest reason is that the same car left Pennsylvania only last month, and it was one of the only cars that made it out of the holding area on the border. So, with transportation, and the time it would take to getting it torn apart to retrieve the money, and then fixed and reconditioned, it could only possibly have been finished sometime last week; which, I might add, is still a pretty darn fast turnaround."

Both Jim and Danielle reply, "That's the Manheim way, everything gets done in a week."

Marnia says, "We don't think they are being held somewhere else other than Maximillian's main compound. Max has a company in Guatemala that has a private prison contract. It is located near Quetzaltenango, just off Guatemala Highway CA1 that joins Mexico Highway 190. This is part of the southerly trucking route used to cross Mexico into Central America. Basically, he provides a prison for the state to send its convicts to, and then he has the privilege of using them for slave labor. He also uses that facility to house many of his own people who have been caught and prosecuted, or who he wants to punish himself. It is a pretty profitable business for him, and it's not just Guatemala that uses him, but Mexico, Honduras, and Belize too."

"So, what makes you so sure my family is there?" says Jim.

Chuck continues for Marnia, "Well, Jim, that's where the Manerez Cartel is having their cars shipped to from Boris's operation."

Marnia adds, "If you think about it, it's the perfect place. For one, there is a huge decommissioned military base right next to Max's prison that he also owns. It has a very large motor pool facility. Two and a half years ago they renovated it into a huge auto reconditioning center not unlike your own right here, Jim."

"So, for three years Mom, Daddy, and Grandma have been prisoners down there with no communication with the outside world. Those bastards," Danielle says as the tears roll down her cheeks.

"I am no fan of Maximillian Manerez. He is a cold-blooded killer, and one of the most ruthless men alive, but he also saved your family's lives when Boris tried to kill them." Marnia tries to console Danielle.

Jim holds up both hands in an attention gesture. "Okay, whatever the details are, one thing is for sure. We need to get my wife, son, and daughter-in-law back as soon as possible."

Marnia starts to lay out a plan to do just that.

Next Day, Roberto's Office at Jacob's Ladder South Texas

Roberto is still getting used to the fact that Danielle now lives back in Manheim, Pennsylvania with her paternal grandfather. He loved having Danielle live in South Texas for a few years, but he prayed and believed for this to happen someday because he knew that's where she needed to be. But he still misses that little fireball.

Alyeks Yeshlton, the renowned Russian dance instructor, and his wife Patti bought a house and moved into the area about two weeks ago. He told Roberto that the hospital might let him move his sick brother in with them if he can prove he can provide the right care. In light of that, Isabella is with them, helping the couple plan a room that will accommodate Alyeks's brother.

The cell phone rings and Roberto smiles because it's Danielle. "Hi, Grandpa, I hope you are sitting because I have some pretty serious news I need to discuss with you, and it is going to be quite a shock." Danielle goes on to tell her grandpa, her mother's dad, that Mary, Jacob, and Linda are still alive and being held prisoner at a jail in Guatemala. She slowly and methodically fills him in on every detail, including Marnia's plan to rescue the trio. At first Roberto can't believe what he is hearing, but as Danielle continues to fill him in on all the details, it finally hits him that his little girl Mary and the rest are still alive.

"*Oh, gracias a Dios*— it is a fantastic miracle. I don't even know what to say."

Danielle tells him that she and Jim are leaving right away for South Texas and that she will see him soon. Of course, Roberto insists on being a part of the whole rescue operation.

Office of Rear Admiral James Harrington USCG Retired, CEO of Harrington Enterprises

James is a little flustered that no one from Boris's side of the operation has contacted him yet. Of course, Boris is in custody in a Mexican prison and most likely going to be executed for his infamous crime, but in his way of thinking, there had to be a number of people in Boris's operation who would want to keep things going. James did not have a shipping network set up to safely bring cartel money down south of the border like Boris, but he did have a very elaborate and, in his own opinion, very secure conventional money laundering operations that charged only thirty-five percent off the top. And for the last month, business had been very good.

James's cell phone rings and he immediately recognizes the number. "Yes, son, what is it? I told you to call me only if there's an emergency."

"Dad, I have been cooped up here in Max's hacienda on Falcon Lake for a month now. What are we going to do to get me back to the States?"

"Now, son, you know the only way we could keep the heat off Harrington Enterprises is to make the authorities believe you were acting alone on the take, there in Brownsville. The evidence Max planted made them believe that you were connected to Natasha and her crime syndicate in Russia and northern Europe. I have released a statement to the press saying how disappointed I am in you, and that I am imploring you to give yourself up over to the authorities. I have also reached out to Natasha several times also, asking her help in getting you a new identity so that you can come back into the United States safely. These things take time, son. I am sure she is lying low as well. We just need to give it more time."

Will rolls his eyes, knowing that his dad really is the big old blowhard that everyone said he was in the Coast Guard.

"Yes, well that's not the reason I called you, Dad. You see, I heard some of Max's guys talking, and one of them said that they were in the Manerez private prison down in Guatemala for a year and just got out. That he was on a work crew that put the cars back together after they stripped the money out of them. And guess who he said one of his bosses looked like at the shop?"

"Son, how would I know, and why would I possibly care?"

Just the response Will expected, but he's sure his next statement will floor his father.

"Dad," he nervously continues, "the man said that he was sure it was the Hero of Cozumel, Jacob Edwards."

Momentarily stunned, James quickly regains his composure and says, "That's simply absurd, son, there is no chance that could even be remotely possible."

"I don't know dad, you remember that stuff about the three people who were taken off the plane? Why did Max have us use our contacts in L.A. to cover that up?"

He rolls his eyes at his son's lack of seeing the simple obvious. "It's just like he said. Anything that would prolong the investigation could turn up something that could point to him and his organization. Boris was very clear that we gave Maximillian any and all help that he requested. Helping him close the investigation was part of that deal. Besides Will, you and I made a nice little bonus when we took that three million off the top of the ten Boris gave us for bribe money."

"Okay, Dad, but it just occurred to me that if Max ever wanted to have a trump card he could use against Boris someday, keeping Jacob and his family secretly hostage would be the best one."

James puts his hand to his forehead, and rolls his eyes. "That's why you leave the big thinking to me, Will. You've always had an overactive imagination." James hangs up the phone with a promise that he will reach out to Natasha unceasingly until she helps him get a new identity.

Harrington's intercom buzzes. The receptionist down stairs says, "Mr. Harrington, I have a Mr. Robert Malcolm here from Lancaster, Pennsylvania. He says he is the attorney representing the Yuri Sebastion Estate. Also, a Deputy Director Chuck Yeager of the FBI is with him. Shall I send them up?"

The news makes him giddy with anticipation. He has been waiting for Natasha to reach out to him and knows this must be how she is going to do it. "By all means, send them both right up."

He wishes that he were the major shareholder in the company that bears his name. But if truth be told, he only owns twenty percent of the stock and he is still paying Boris back for the loan to purchase that. The other eighty percent was in that sniveling little weasel Yuri's name. The biggest favor Boris ever did for him was to kill that little idiot on the cruise ship. He still seethes every time he recalls Yuri's last visit. That little maggot walked into his office like he owned the place and actually had the gall to tell him get out from behind his own desk, that he had work to do for Boris and needed some privacy.

With Yuri gone he is convinced Natasha will treat him with the respect he deserves.

Robert Malcolm and Chuck Yeager knock on the door and James lets the pair in. Mr. Malcolm enters first followed by a middle-aged blond-haired man who seems familiar. He shakes their hands and says to Chuck, "Have we met Deputy Director Yeager?"

Chuck can't hide his grin. He has been looking forward to this little meeting for a while now. "As a matter of fact, we met in Sector Corpus Christi back in the late nineties. I was part of a special pirate task force down there when I was active duty in the Coast Guard."

The color drains from James's face as he plops down in his seat. "That's right, I remember. You and Jacob Edwards joined up after graduating from Kings Point. You both showed high aptitudes in law enforcement and investigation, that is why we put you in that task force after your initial assignments. I had no idea you went into the FBI after your service in the Coast Guard."

Chuck gleefully decides to prolong the stress and presses, "Yes, as I remember, you were adamantly against forming that task force in the Caribbean at the time. I believe you said, 'That stuff just doesn't happen that much down there. We need to use our resources elsewhere.' It's a good thing the commandant didn't listen to you, or incidents like Falcon Lake, Cozumel, and a few others would have been disasters."

Harrington's eyes seethe in anger and reveal he'd like nothing more than to see Yeager melt in front of him.

Chuck matches the intensity of Harrington's glare and says, "You know, that look worked really well on a couple of junior grade lieutenants about twenty years ago, but I am a Deputy Director of the FBI, and you're just an old blowhard who has been on the take for a long time."

Harrington springs to his feet with his accusing finger wagging in Chuck's face. "You have no right to talk to me like that, you little punk."

"You know," Chuck says truly enjoying the moment, "if it's the last thing I do, I'm going to pin Cozumel and that plane explosion on you and your mealy-mouthed worm of a son. Don't think that we don't know that Maximillian is hiding him over at his Falcon Lake hacienda, because we do. The only one who kept us away from figuring all this stuff out was Boris."

Harrington's nervousness begins to seep into his eyes.

"Yes," Chuck continues, "Boris was good, but Mexico's got him now, and you and your son are mine. I am going to leave you and Danielle's attorney alone, to talk over the future of her company. Do not leave the state, Harrington. You are now a suspect in a major FBI investigation, and we are watching you very closely. Oh, and I wouldn't try to call any of your old friends in Washington for help, if I were you. Your former boss, the vice president of the United States, has already informed every one of them to back off and have no contact with you. You might want to get ready for prison life."

Harrington, stunned, drops back into his seat. Chuck pauses to relish the victory and nod his head in triumph. After a few seconds he shakes Mr. Malcolm's hand, thanks him, and leaves.

Robert Malcolm has been Jim Edwards' attorney for longer than he can remember. He considers Jim one of his closest friends and he always treated Linda, Jacob, Mary, and Danielle like family. After Chuck Yeager fully briefed him on how the FBI was closing in on the Harringtons, he decided to have Chuck accompany him to the meeting, at least the first part. He knew he could not allow Chuck to stay for the rest, where he had the privilege of telling James Harrington where he stands in his company, but he knew that Chuck already understood the details and didn't necessarily have to see Robert lower the boom on the guy, although he really would have enjoyed it.

"Mr. Harrington, I represent Mr. Yuri Sebastion's widow, Danielle Sebastion." James, still reeling from the encounter with Chuck Yeager, barely hears Robert; but the impact of Mr. Malcolm's words begins to sink in.

"Danielle? What could Danielle possibly have to do with my company? I...did you say "Danielle SEBASTION? Yuri's widow?"

Robert is quite amused as he sees the dark illumination take form in Harrington's already disfigured face.

"That is correct, Mr. Harrington. Before he died, Danielle and Yuri were legally wed last month on a yacht cruise in South Texas off the coast of the South Padre Islands."

James tries to hold himself together and just can't as he blurts out, "That was all just a farce, wasn't it? Boris Rasmov forced Danielle to marry Yuri in a plot to control Edwards Auto through that marriage."

Robert opens up his briefcase, takes out some paperwork along with a legal pad, and starts to write down some notes. "It's odd that you are so knowledgeable of the motive behind the wedding. I don't believe those details have been released to the media, or anyone else outside the immediate families. Would you care to enlighten me as to how you came to understand these details?"

James Harrington, not a young man anymore, was warned by his doctor to not get himself all worked up over business. He reaches over, grabs some carbonated water and a couple of prescription tranquilizers, pops them in his mouth, and takes a long swig from the plastic bottle. "What does this have to do with my company, Harrington Enterprises?"

"Well, for starters, the new owner of this financial institution does not want to call it Harrington Enterprises any more, nor does she want its current management to remain in control of the company."

James, despite his best efforts to regain control of himself and remain calm, jumps out of his seat and points a trembling finger at Robert. "Look you backwoods carpetbagger, I own twenty percent of this institution and the people behind Sebastion Auto are the Rasmov family. I am confident that they will not allow this little debutante from Edwards Auto come in here and take over everything."

Robert is amused at how unhinged James has become and thinks, *I haven't had this much fun in a long time.*

"Well," Robert continues, "It may surprise you to know that the Rasmov family from Russia authorized Boris to transfer all their U.S. companies over to Mr. and Mrs. Yuri Sebastion as a wedding gift. If you look here, we have all the paperwork notarized and formally submitted to the proper agencies. As for your twenty percent, the new owner of the institution called in your debt, and took payment in the form of stocks you had in the company, as per your signed contract and agreement with the Rasmovs. So, that brings your holdings of this institution down to two point five percent, which has been frozen pending an FBI investigation into any and all dealings done by Harrington Enterprises since its inception twelve years ago."

James Harrington, in a state of shock unlike any he has ever experienced, grabs his carbonated water, finishes the bottle, and throws it in the trash. With the best composure he can muster in the circumstances, he says, "What is Danielle going to call *my* company now?"

Robert pulls out a few more papers and pretends to read something. "Well, they are still kicking that one around but right now the most popular is B&YBM."

"Really?" James says leaning back in the chair that is not his anymore. "What the hell does that mean?"

"Boris & Yuri's Big Mistake." Robert tries but can't hold in his chuckle.

*   *   *

One hour later, James Harrington, former CEO of a financial institution that once bore his name, walks out of his former office carrying a few personal items in a box. As he walks through the main office area, he sees about a dozen FBI people talking to his former staff, looking at the computers, and digging through all his file cabinets.

Chuck Yeager returns to Harrington's former office. He knows it's just a matter of time before he finds the safe that holds all the illicit activity and money laundering details—and when he does, all hell is going to break loose.

Chapter Three

Force of Nature

Manerez Maximum Security Prison, Guatemala Present Day

Mary Edwards is feeling almost normal now that she can do just about everything she is used to doing. The medication she was on really did help her get through most of the pregnancy without the horrible bedridden ordeal she went through the first time. The last month of the pregnancy was a bit rougher though, and Dr. Chavez upped the medication and insisted on a c-section delivery. Mary had to laugh at herself now, remembering how indignant she felt when he told her that she could not have the baby naturally. Just one look at little Roberto, and she knew that it was all worth it, and her doctor was absolutely right. Roberto was a fine looking toddler of two-and-a-half years old now. He had his father's eyes along with his unlimited stamina. Mary could think of nothing more appropriate than naming her first boy after her father, and Jacob felt the same way, so they chose the name Roberto James Edwards. She swells with pride as she looks adoringly at this little miracle playing in the sand box behind their little cottage in the staff section of the prison.

The work horn blasts across the compound. Through the fence she sees that the men are done working over in the automotive reconditioning center and are heading back toward the main grounds. She stands and picks up little Roberto. "Daddy is coming. Let's go greet him, okay?" Mary gives him a high five as they walk out to the front of the cottage on the main road into the complex.

Roberto smiles and giggles, bounces up and down in Mary's arms, and says, "Daddy!" At the end of the road to Mary's right, the big gate swings open and several armed guards line up on either side as over one hundred men begin to file back into the prison grounds. Mary is standing on her tip toes with her free hand shading the glare of the sun from her eyes as she finally spots Jacob and Jonathan walking back from work. She waves and they both wave back.

It's been a ten-hour day reconditioning the vehicles. Both men are bone-tired but very satisfied from a good, solid day of production. About a year ago, Jonathan took a big interest in the restoration of the cars and started working with Jacob on every aspect of reconditioning and reselling them. Jacob was pretty impressed with this billionaire's son, who had never really had to do an honest day's work in his life, but now was putting in ten-hour days and was learning not only dealership wholesales, but body work and detailing.

Jacob is eager to hug his wife and hold his son after such an exhausting day at work. "Well, this is about the most beautiful sight I have seen all day. @ Jacob hugs and kisses his wife and grabs his son from her arms. Little Roberto just giggles and gives his daddy a big hug and kiss as he motions to the back yard where he wants his dad to play with him.

"You two go ahead." Mary says, "I will help Linda finish with supper, but both of you are taking a good shower before we eat, okay?"

Jacob looks over at his friend. "Jonathan, if you would like to hang around for dinner, you are more than welcome. Mary can you grab us a couple of beers?"

Jonathan laughs as he responds. "Jacob, I am just as dirty as you are, and I don't think we can all get a shower in before Mary and Linda get supper ready. Besides, my father flew in this afternoon and he has something urgent he needs to talk to me about, so I will have to take a rain check."

Mary reaches out and places a hand on Jonathan's shoulder. "Well, you are always welcome, and Linda loves to make too much food anyway. Please, tell your father we would like to have an update on Jim and Danielle when possible." Jonathan assures them both that he will get any info his father has on the rest of their family and let them know as soon as he can. He says goodbye and walks back to the main building where he and his father's private apartments are.

Jonathan Manerez has grown quite attached to the Edwards trio since their kidnapping three years ago. Commander Jacob Edwards, the Hero of Cozumel, had been his hero for a long time now. The only man ever to defeat Dominik Thrace, and the man that saved the life of the woman he loved, Marnia Gonzalez, The Cartel Crusher. Jonathan remembers that the moment he saw the trio in the prison hospital after the plane crash that he would do everything in his power to protect them from his father and from Boris. Not telling Marnia about them being alive was destroying him on the inside but he really had no choice. With Boris still out there, and knowing how ruthless his father could be, keeping it secret from her was his only option right now.

The Edwards have no idea that it was Jonathan's idea to let them have the kind of freedom they have enjoyed for their stay in his father's prison. If Maximillian had his way, they would all three have basically existed in a dungeon without even seeing daylight. Jonathan's relationship with his father has always been strained and complicated. His mother was a singer from Los Angeles, California. Maximillian became obsessed with her. He went to L.A., met her, and had a torrid affair with her. She was only partially aware that he was a notorious criminal.

She became pregnant with Jonathan almost immediately. Three months after giving birth to him Max brought her to Mexico and put her under house arrest keeping her that way until she tried to escape with her four-year-old son. After he and his mother were caught and returned to the hacienda, his mother was taken to see his father. He remembers how terrified she looked as the men took her away from him. That was the last time Jonathan ever saw his mother. No one, including Max, would ever even let him talk about her again.

Jonathan was taken to another ranch in southern Mexico where he met the woman whom Max insisted was now his mother. He lived with this very cold and quiet woman for another ten years until his father brought him to his prison to start showing him the business. At age seventeen, Max sent him off to college in Spain where he studied international law and business.

Jonathan later found out that his father's wife was the daughter of a very powerful general in South America, on whom he relied deeply to do business in that region. She was also barren and never gave his father an heir. The general insisted that Max not take any other wives and that his daughter would be taken care of for the rest of her life. According to the Mexican birth certificate, Jonathan was the son of Maximillian Manerez and his wife.

For a while, Jonathan fell into the role of being a cartel leader's son, ruthless, ambitious, and totally loyal to his father. He was forced to do a lot of things that he was not very proud of, and after a time it started to eat at him. Jonathan discovered that he had a conscience. He started showing mercy to people that Max wanted punished or killed. Then he met Captain Marnia Gonzalez of the Mexican Anti-Cartel Task Force. He helped her take down a number of cartels, including the powerful Santiago Cartel, and fell in love with her.

Although he successfully convinced his father that he was *using her* to build leverage, position, and build their cartel, he felt it tenuous at best maintaining the illusion. That's also when Max put him in charge of the prison. He thought it would harden his son and make him into the heir he expected someday. But making him responsible for the Edwards was doing just the opposite.

He knows he can never tell Marnia that Jacob is alive and is his father's prisoner. She would, without doubt, no relationship withstanding, attack the place with anything and everything she could muster and probably get everyone killed. Knowing what he knows has put a huge strain on his relationship with Marnia. True, he helped her to clean up some ruthless gangs that operated on the Guatemalan-Mexican border, but still, in the last year they have seen less and less of each other. The guilt of keeping the Edwards secret from her is taxing. Over the last three years he has refused to execute anyone, and refused to oversee his father's cage fights.

Now Max has called him and insisted on this urgent meeting. Jonathan fears the worst. He fears that this meeting will be all about his refusals and his behavior with the Edwards. All these thoughts swirl in his mind as he enters his main living quarters, a luxurious apartment that he sometimes shares with his father when Max is around. Max stands with his back to his son as he looks out over the yard toward the entrance through which he and Jacob had come from the auto recon center.

Max takes a big drag on his Cuban cigar. "You and Jacob have developed quite a little business together. I think in a couple of years, it could rival Jacob's father's profit don't you?"

The sarcasm is not lost on Jonathan, "I know that the profit we are making off the refurbished vehicles is nothing compared to the cartel, Father. But don't you think it's a great way to get rid of the junk, keep prisoners occupied, and make something profitable out of these pieces of metal? I thought you would be pleased that nothing in this operation from beginning to end is unprofitable. While the rest of the idiots just scrap the smuggling cars at huge loss, we are actually selling for a profit."

Turning around with deliberate purpose he steps toward his only son and gets sternly in his face. "You are a very talented business man, son. You have the makings of a better cartel leader than me, but you have lost your killer instinct. I put you here to get it back, not to become an automobile wholesaler. Anyway, that is not why I am here. We have a very big problem with Boris and his operation." Jonathan sees the fear in his father's eyes and knows that Boris is one of the few men in the world that can generate such concern in his father. "What is going on, Father? We just received nine hundred million dollars last month and are expecting the next shipment in a few days?"

Max sits back down and sighs and says. "That's the problem; the next shipment is not coming. Half of it has been confiscated by that little bitch Captain Marnia Gonzalez and the other half by the FBI. To make matters worse, Marnia has arrested Boris and is holding him in a secret maximum security fortress right now. He is to be charged with a myriad of crimes, not the least of which is the murder of Jacob Edwards, his mother, and his wife."

Jonathan is stunned to the core, and feels a deep panic of concern for his friend Jacob and his family, which he cannot afford to let his father know. "With that label on Boris's head," Jonathan says, "he might not make it out of any Mexican prison alive. That is why you keep Jacob here instead of anywhere in Mexico. He is too popular, and his face is just too well known. How did this all happen, Father? I thought Boris was the most untouchable man alive?"

Max looks deeply into his son's eyes trying to discern a hint of sarcasm, but can find only genuine concern and a little fear, which Max is relieved to see. "It is these damn Edwards. They are like a force of nature. Sometimes I feel that the elements themselves favor them. Boris thought that it was finally time to eliminate Jim and Danielle. When his plan to kill everyone except Danielle failed, it took him up until now to instigate a new plan where he would manipulate a marriage between Danielle and his nephew Yuri. His daughter, Natasha, asked me to put together a crew of would-be pirates and outfit an old cutter to sail north up the Mexican Coast and meet him on his rented yacht just south of the Padre Islands."

Max draws on his cigar, folds his arms enjoying the rich flavor, and thinks for a second before continuing. "Everything was going as planned perfectly, but someone tipped off the FBI in Philadelphia and helped them discover Boris's whole operation in Manheim, Pennsylvania. And then somehow, Marnia Gonzalez got involved, and so did that bastard Major John Brown of the Texas Rangers. After that, it was like the whole law enforcement world of Mexico and the United States was dead set on saving Jim and Danielle Edwards. The Coast Guard disabled and captured my cutter before it could meet up with Boris, and Marnia and another Coast Guard patrol boat saved the rented yacht before Boris's daughter Natasha could destroy it with her father's private yacht. Boris did not even have the satisfaction of seeing our people assassinate that annoying retired Coast Guard chief and his family at the hospital. And not only was that family saved, but John Brown was able to capture the team I sent to Starr County Hospital to kill that turncoat who is testifying against us next month."

Jonathan sits in a chair next to his father trying to comprehend what this all means. "But Father, none of this really explains how Danielle and Jim survived. I have never heard of Boris letting any of his victims get away, except, of course, Jacob."

Max nods.

Jonathan takes a deep breath. "My God, Father, this is all so incredible."

Max takes another long drag on his cigar as he reaches for his glass of tequila. After a swig, he looks at his son and says, "Exactly."

Max goes on to tell his son what they have been able to piece together of what happened on that cruise ship that night. Jonathan can't help himself when he starts to chuckle emphatically.

"Father, I'm sorry to laugh, but what you're saying is that that Rasmovs tried to kill the Edwards, and the Edwards beat the crap out of both of them for it?"

Max practically chokes on the mouthful of tequila he is trying to swallow. "That's not even the best part. While the United States and Mexican officials argued on the yacht about who gets Boris, Jim Edwards grabbed him by the collar and handcuffs, walked him to the edge of the deck, and literally threw him some fifteen feet onto Captain Marnia Gonzalez's boat. He then congratulated her on a fine arrest."

Jonathan, in mid-swig, laughs uncontrollably with his father, splashing beer on himself and the floor. They speak a few minutes more, then Max excuses himself to go check on some prisoners he is having disciplined by his managers. Jonathan is relieved that Max can't decide what to do with Jacob and his family. So many things revolve around this private prison of the Manerez Cartel. Jonathan knows that his father's idea in taking over and running this prison was quite a flash of genius—the perfect tool to motivate his underlings and to keep all the different elements of the Manerez Cartel in line.

After discussing the botched yacht incident and how Danielle and Jim Edwards had prevailed over Boris and Natasha, Max opened up about his phobia of Jacob Edwards. He reminisced about how Dominik Thrace, the undefeated cage fighting champion, was so easily bested and executed by Jacob those many years ago. One of Santiago's best assassins, Dominik was an uncontrollable beast who felt he had the right to rape and pillage anywhere he wanted.

Jonathan also shudders remembering that during Dominik's stay at the prison, he killed everyone he encountered in the cage fight ring. Max told him that he never saw a fighter like that wild man, almost bestial. Everyone was afraid of him, including Max. That is why he talked Santiago into selling him to Boris in the first place. It was either that or execute the animal. When he and Santiago heard that the Coast Guard Commander Jacob Edwards easily destroyed the Jamaican monster in hand-to-hand combat, they could not believe it was true until they checked out the story for themselves with some of the parents of the girls who were there. Also, the surviving Mexican security specialist saw the whole thing and gave a firsthand account. Jacob went into that kitchen office unarmed and alone and when he emerged from the kitchen, he was dragging the broken, semiconscious, half dead Jamaican by his braided hair.

Jonathan recognized that Max had rarely spoken to Jacob during the Edwards' stay at the prison, and when he did, he kept his distance. Jacob told Jonathan about the finance minister's yacht that he and his friend Chuck Yeager boarded off the coast of Honduras in '96, and what they found inside. Jonathan knew that it was Dominik that had murdered the finance minister and raped that girl and often thought about telling Jacob that the man he killed in Cozumel was the same man that was responsible for the horror on that boat. But Maximillian had thought about it too and forbad Jonathan to ever tell Jacob any of those things. But one thing was for sure, Jonathan knew he couldn't fault Jacob for what drove him to be so formidable at times and to punish these vile abusers.

Edwards Cottage that Night

Linda, Mary, Jacob, and little Roberto sit around the table for their evening meal. Jacob and Roberto are clean and fresh after their showers. Roberto loves it when his dad puts a dab of shaving cream on his tiny face and lets him use the blunt side of a comb to shave it off while daddy trims his own beard with a pair of scissors. Mary spots a little excess cream on Roberto's ear and wipes it off. She motions Jacob to do the same to his own ear. They hold hands and Mary says a prayer of thanks for the meal and adds an extra request to keep Danielle, both Grandpas, Jim and Roberto, her mother Isabella, and her brothers safe and blessed. They say amen and begin to eat.

Mary asks the same question she always asks, "Did you hear any updates on what Danielle and the others are doing, darling?" Jacob usually does not have much to tell but today he heard, in his opinion, some really juicy news about their daughter.

"Well, apparently our daughter went out on a date recently with someone we both know really well."

Jacob slowly takes another bite of his mother's delicious chicken dinner, enjoying withholding the details and dragging it out. He picks up his beer for a sip and feels a hot roll hit him on the side of his head. Linda sternly looks at Jacob. "Stop clowning around, little boy. Who'd she go out with?"

He feels the imprint of his wife's fist in his shoulder. Little Roberto thinks it's a food fight and throws mashed potatoes at his grandmother. Jacob finds that so funny he almost falls off his chair laughing hysterically.

Mary jumps up and grabs little Roberto before he can throw anymore food. "Please, Jacob! Just tell us who she went out with?"

"Okay, okay," Jacob says, as he settles himself down and endeavors to clean the mashed potatoes off his mother. "Do you remember Christopher Rottanelli, the boy I helped get into Kings Point? He worked at the shop one summer, and Mary and I took him to the All Academy Ball at the Union League in Philadelphia his last year." Mary and Linda both say they remember him. Jacob continues. "Well, he just made full lieutenant this past year and was transferred to Station Brazos this summer to command the security patrol boat recently stationed there."

Mary is intrigued by the news. "So that's how Danielle met him. I don't think she would readily remember him. She was in eighth grade when he worked at the shop and I believe that was the summer she spent most of her time with you, Linda. Is that right?"

Linda pokes her chin with her right index finger pondering for a moment. "That's right, because that summer Danielle learned how to do payroll, and vehicle registrations." Mary smiles from ear to ear as she exclaims, "I really liked that boy! Good student, hard worker, and nice gentleman. I approve."

Jacob laughs. "Well, I hope he kept in contact with Dad because you know Roberto is going to put him through the third degree and Dad was the only one who could help me when it came to your very protective old man, Mary."

Mary sighs. "Well, my father is a very good judge of character and I am sure he will see what a fine young man Christopher is." She looks over at Linda and giggles. "But getting some advice from Jim couldn't hurt. There probably wasn't a boy in South Texas who was not a little intimidated by my dad when it came to asking me out."

Linda chuckles. "Yes, and that includes my little boy who could not help but put his foot in his mouth every time he talked to Roberto back then."

Jacob looks at these two women who always seem to get the upper hand in everything lately, turns his attention to his son, and says, "How about a little help here, buddy? I am outgunned on every side?"

Little Roberto looks at everyone rather sternly, grabs his sippy cup and pounds it on the table as he says, "Danielle *my* sister. Who is Tistofer?" The whole table explodes in laughter as they continue their meal together.

As Jonathan approaches the Edwards' cottage, he hears all the jovial laughter coming from within and can't help but be a little jealous of the family atmosphere that just permeates from this group. Granted, he actually has had some nice times with his father like the one he just experienced laughing and joking about Boris getting his ass kicked. But, there is always an underlying tone of disapproval coming from his father that he never can quite get past. Jonathan is taking a huge risk going to Jacob so soon with the information he just learned from his father, but deep in his gut he knows it is the right thing to do.

Jacob knocks three times fast and two times slow on the front door and he hears Jacob bellow, "Come in." It was the prearranged knock that they had set up so the Edwards would know it was him. Jonathan greets everyone within.

Jacob grins, "Did you change your mind about dinner? You must have smelled Mom's chicken and come running."

Jonathan gazes at this family that he has given himself to protect from his father these last almost three years and feels a pang of guilt for having a part in their bad circumstances. "No, Jacob. Although it does smell delicious, I need to talk to you about some problems I am having in the merchandise retrieval from the vehicles as they come in. Do you have a moment?" Jonathan motions to meet him outside.

More code. Jacob knows it means that Jonathan has something serious he needs to talk about. Jacob established that he would have nothing to do with getting the illicit money out of the vehicles. He has, however, made suggestions on how to cause less damage to the vehicles in the process. But the code was setup so they would know when they need to talk in private.

Jacob gets up, excuses himself, and walks out the back door over to Roberto's sandbox where they both know there are no hidden mics or direct surveillance cameras. Standing out in the quiet Jonathan tells Jacob to just listen. "Boris made his move on Jim, Danielle, and on Roberto and his family and failed." Jacob immediately stiffens in alarm, but Jonathan puts his hand on his friend's shoulder and says, "Don't worry, everyone is safe. Marnia Gonzalez has arrested Boris and he is now a prisoner of the Mexican Anti-Cartel Task Force. Although this is very good news for your family in Pennsylvania and Texas, it also means that your lives are at risk here. My father has not decided what to do with you, but I feel like he is leaning on eliminating all of you. I'm going to help you in any way I can, but we need to be careful. He does not fully trust me and I am probably being followed as we speak. So, let's just go back into the house and finish the conversation we were having about retrieving the money from the cars as we walk out front. Jacob nods his head and starts to walk back in with his friend, and now ally.

* * *

Jonathan wakes up the next morning after a fitful sleep filled with nightmares of the last time he saw his mother. He calls to the main office and they inform him that his father spent the whole night running cage fights with some of the more volatile inmates, and running the betting pit where online subscribers could bet on the competitors. Jonathan had not run one of those matches for over two years and told his father he was much too busy handling the vehicles and the money they brought to be doing anything like that.

He pointed out that every time he took a day off to run cage fights, they actually lost money compared to what they made with Jacob's contribution to the business. His father did not like it, but Maximillian Manerez always sided with the logic that produced the most profit, and his son knew that quite well. He just got dressed and went to work with Jacob. He knew it would be way after 3:00 p.m. before his father was up and ready to see him. He intended to use that time to save his friend and friend's family.

Jacob knows he cannot say anything to his wife or mom just yet. He needs to develop a plan with Jonathan and be fully prepared to implement it when the time comes. He walks out of the apartment and over to the gate with the rest of the prisoner's ready to go to work. Jonathan steps out of his living area with the usual contingent of guards to escort the group to the motor pool auto recon center. Jonathan and Jacob meet up at the gate.

Jacob smiles and says, "Morning, boss, ready for another hot one?"

Jonathan nods his head. "That's all we ever get down here are hot ones, but it never stops you from saying it." They both chuckle at the old joke and proceed to work.

The whole complex is bugged and monitored by his father's people at a remote location, but he is confident that he and Jacob can talk in the detail shop. The background noise is so intense in there with power washers, vacuum cleaners, buffers, polishers, and air compressors going all at the same time that you can hardly hear yourself think. A year ago Jacob came up with the great idea of using noise suppression ear muffs. Mostly used when firing guns, they drown out loud background noise, but make it possible for two people to talk to one another while on the range. The muffs Jonathan purchased were small enough to look like regular shop earmuffs. He brought them back with him from a trip to Mexico City after seeing Marnia sometime ago. He then made a bulk order of regular muffs that looked just like his and Jacobs. Everyone in the shop wore them, so no one observing a surveillance video would be able to tell the difference. Standing next to each other with all that noise, they hear each other as if talking in a quiet room.

They are both on the opposite side of a big black suburban buffing out the paint work done the day before in the body shop. "So, you think we have to move pretty quickly?" Jacob asks as he is buffing the hood.

"Yes, I think that my father will try to have you all killed tonight, though he has said nothing to me of his plans. I do have some people who I can trust, and I think that if we can make some kind of distraction at the end of the day, we can steal a truck and make our way to the coast where I can get a boat to take us up the Pacific coast to Los Angeles."

Jacob says, "If we can get in Mexican waters and you have a good radio or cell service, I have a friend in the Mexican military who will help us, if I can convince her it's me."

"Are you referring to Captain Marnia Gonzalez? I had some-one send her a message early this morning. We should be able to count on the help you are talking about at the right time."

Jonathan explains his escape plan to Jacob. He's arranged for a couple prisoners that are loyal to him to help out. While Jacob is walking back to his cottage from work, they will attack Jacob under the pretense that they are seeking revenge for what he did to Frankie. Jacob needs to make the fight last as long as possible while Jonathan gets a SUV and discreetly retrieves Linda, Mary, and little Roberto. He will then park the vehicle close to the com-motion and get the guards to rescue Jacob. Jonathan will step in and announce that he is taking Jacob to the medical facility to have him checked out. The guards will then reopen the gate for them and they will escape to the Pacific coast where Jonathan has a boat waiting. Jacob nods that he understands the plan and silently says a prayer that everything will work out to get him and his family to safety.

Jacob tries to get good sleep that night, but the anticipation keeps him up part of the night. The next day at work things seem a little tense to him but he carries on through the day. The horn blows and as he and Jonathan walk through the gate at the end of the day Jonathan motions with his chin to three big guys on his right. Jacob understands that Jonathan is showing him his would-be sparring partners, and readies himself for the attack. He does not wait long. One of them slams into his back and pushes him to the ground hard.

"You hurt our friend Frankie, now we hurt you, gringo."

He kicks Jacob in the gut but covertly pulls back at the last second. It still hurts like hell, but it was not a full on kick. He's always been able to come up with fighting strategy quickly, and decides that Judo and Aikido are his best bet to prolong this "show fight" without really hurting anyone.

First, he grabs the guy's foot and sucks it into his midsection and uses his elbow to bend the knee in a normal way, so as to not really hurt him. Then, from down on his knees, he pushes his shoulder into the man's butt and lower back making him stumble and fall face first into the dirt. From his kneeling position, he kip-ups to a stand and catches the next guy throwing a haymaker at his head, grabs the hand with his right, twists it around and up so that the palm is facing the man's shoulder, uses his other arm to force the man to the ground and pops him lightly in the head. He pulls the punch so it looks harder than it is. The next guy grabs Jacob by the throat, so he takes his left hand and wraps it around his right wrist, at the same time arching his right arm over the man's head and locking his hand at his collar with his arm and hand. He acts like he is elbowing the man in the head several times, then sucks the man's head into his armpit by arching his arm back around the guys head, pulls up with his upper body, and sits down rolling the man over his front shoulder and onto the ground. Jacob twists his body around so that he is kneeling beside the man ready to punch him in the face. *I hope Jonathan hurries up*, he thinks, *I don't know how long I can keep this up without hurting one of these guys.*

He then sees a black Chevy Suburban pull up and Jonathan get out. He looks at the guards and says, "What are you doing? Break this fiasco up and put these cabrónes in maximum security. I'm taking Jacob to the infirmary to have Dr. Chavez check him out."

"I don't think that there is any need for that. Jacob looks just fine to me." Maximillian walks up with several armed guards all pointing their weapons at Jacob and Jonathan. "You really disappoint me, son. I thought you were made of tougher stuff than this." Max looks over at Jacob and sneers. "That little production was quite entertaining, Jacob, but you must remember I have been running cage fights here in this facility for a long time and I can spot combatants faking a mile away."

Max turns his attention to the three guys who just danced with Jacob. "As for you three cabrónes, as my son said, first you're going to maximum security and then you are going to find out what it is like to really fight for your lives. Tomorrow you will fight each other to the death in the cage."

The biggest one steps forward and defiantly spits on the ground in front of Max. "Ha. What are you but a petty criminal? We were helping the Hero of Cozumel and his family. My life has some meaning now. I do not care what you do to me." He crosses his arms and glares at Maximillian with defiance and disgust, then his two friends join him. A stunned hush settles over the whole crowd as the revelation of Jacob's true identity is revealed to the whole yard. Even the guards are taken aback by the news.

Max fearing he is about to lose control of the situation, grabs a guard's gun and aims it at Jacob. "I will show you that this *hero* of yours is nothing but flesh and blood and can die just like the rest of you."

"No, Father!" Jonathan lunges at Max but in mid-stride, a huge explosion rocks the yard, then another. A guard pushes Jonathan back as Max spins toward the direction of the explosions and horror grips his heart. The building where they store the cars that are packed with smuggled money is blowing to pieces. Everyone stares in shock for what seems like ten seconds when a third and final explosion brings the whole structure down.

Chapter Four

Tommy's Team

Dining Room of Jacob's Ladder, One Day Prior

Danielle is still in a state of both shock and euphoria at the news of her parents and grandmother. She is sitting in a meeting with Jim, Roberto, Isabella, Chuck Yeager, Captains Marnia Gonzalez, Larry Phillips, and Alex Maelstrom, and with Lieutenant Chris Rottanelli, Major John Brown, and a mysterious older military type that no one but Chuck Yeager and the Coast Guard people seem to know. Chuck is showing everyone an aerial photograph of Maximilian's prison and decommissioned military base.

"As you can all see, the prison is very large, but we believe that Jacob, Mary, and Linda are all housed here in the staff section. There is only one entrance to the facility from that side, and it opens out to the newly refurbished auto recon center. We've had people spying on the facility for several days now and have established a schedule for the men who work there. They head to the gate in the staff section accompanied by armed guards at 7:00 a.m. local time and leave at 5:30 p.m. There are two major holding areas for the vehicles; we will call them Extraction and Recon. Jacob works in Recon, here." Chuck uses his laser pointer to single out the old motor pool area of the base. "Extraction, or where they retrieve smuggled money, is here." He points to a large building to the left of recon that used to house tanks and artillery.

"That is our target. If we can threaten Manerez's money, we will have our distraction. Now, for the operation and extraction of our people, I would like to introduce former SEAL Team Commander, Captain Tommy Williams United States Navy, Retired."

The sixty-something-year-old military type that caught Danielle's attention steps up and shakes Chuck's hand. "Thank you, Deputy Director Yeager. First I have to admit that I never thought I would say this to a bunch of puddle jumpers and their families, but it is one of the biggest honors of my life to be with you all tonight, and to be a part of what is about to happen."

A small chuckle echoes from the Coast Guard personnel in the room accompanied by a couple of eye rolls from the ladies. Marnia is totally confused when she looks over to Danielle for clarification. Danielle smiles, "A *puddle jumper* is the sarcastic term the Navy uses to refer to the Coast Guard, here in the United States."

Tommy clears his throat. "I want to make it clear to everyone in this room that this is not an officially sponsored mission by the United States government. That being said, I have been asked by the president and vice president to give you any and all aid that I can."

Danielle stands up and rather vehemently says, "What do you mean 'not an official mission?' Don't they think three citizens being held prisoner isn't enough cause to get totally involved?"

Ready for this, Tommy tells Danielle that the president has been advised by his security people that there is not enough evidence of Commander Edwards and his family being there to make this official. But once Tommy can prove that they are indeed alive and being held captive, the full force of the United States government will come to bear on Maximillian Manerez and his facility.

Jim stands up and interjects, "So, what you're saying is that you are going to mount a rescue mission and once you see my family is alive, you can call in the cavalry?"

"Pretty much, Mr. Edwards, but I don't plan on going in there alone, at least I hope not."

Captain Larry Phillips stands up and gestures with his hand. "I would like to interject here that the vice president called me today and informed me that any military personnel in this group who would like to volunteer to help Tommy will be given the proper time off and cover needed to do so."

Every hand in the room flies up without hesitation, including retired and nonmilitary personnel. Tommy laughs. "I have to say that after reading the reports of last month's attempt by The Chameleon to kill Jim and Danielle, and how a bunch of you thwarted it, I am not surprised by the enthusiasm. But first, I need people with military training in combat and tactics. A few years back, the department of the Navy started a program where we would offer some of our SEAL training to different military and law enforcement units who might need some of our skill sets. When the pirate incidents started escalating in Somalia and parts of the Caribbean, we were asked to train some Coast Guard people. One of my best and brightest pupils was then Lieutenant Jacob Edwards, and also a pretty wily lieutenant Chuck Yeager, who at the time were part of a pirate task force right in this sector. Since that time, we also had Captain Maelstrom go through the program, and Lieutenant Rottanelli also just finished six months ago. You two plus Captain Gonzalez are my first choice for a rescue team."

Danielle takes a long look at Chris. "Keeping secrets from me, Lieutenant?"

Chris first looks a little nervously around the room at all the brass, and then stares at Tommy and mumbles as he nods his chin in that direction. "Well, he's probably the only guy in the world who wouldn't get court-martialed or arrested for telling you that."

Tommy walks over to Chris and pats him on the back, "He's right, you know. I actually had to ask the secretary of the Navy for permission to tell all of you."

Jim walks over. "I have never been in the military, but I have had some law enforcement training and I am still a certified EMT and fire fighter in the state of Pennsylvania. I think Danielle is still also. We most definitely want to come."

Tommy looks over at Roberto, who affirms with a nod. "The Chief and I talked about that earlier and we agree that you and Danielle should come, but only as drivers, and emergency medical if needed. Roberto, Captain Phillips, and Major John Brown will coordinate with Texas law enforcement to be ready for any backup or contingency plans.

We take two trucks into the compound—Jim and Danielle will be the drivers. Chris and I will go with Danielle, Alex and Marnia will go with Jim. Marnia, you and Alex are going to blow up the extraction facility and then join us at the front gate. Danielle, you're going to wait just outside the compound on the highway while Chris and I sneak in, scale the compound wall, and provide cover when both trucks arrive at the front gate. Alex, when you and Marnia have hit the switch on the explosives in the extraction facility, you head immediately to the front gate, signal Danielle to join you, and Chris and I will figure out how to get the gate opened during the confusion. If you see a bunch of vehicles leaving the front gate, wait till they are out of the way before entering. It will probably be Max's main security force responding to the explosion. That is what I really want to happen because we won't have to deal with them yet. Marnia, can you arrange for equipment and transportation for us when we dock in Livingston?"

Marnia gets a devious grin on her face. "Tommy, that's my playground down there. I can get you anything you want."

Tommy looks at his watch. "Captain Maelstrom's security cutter is docked at Brazos and will leave on its scheduled run to Guatemala Livingston port in five hours. We all need to be on that boat and ready. I will see you then."

As Tommy heads out, Danielle catches up to him and says, "Excuse me, Captain Williams, but can I ask you something?"

Tommy turns around and looks at Danielle. "You know," he says, "I never could decide who you looked more like, your father or your mother." Danielle is a little taken aback because she is sure she has never met this man before. Tommy catches her confusion immediately. "I had your dad for six months of intense training and there was not a day that went by that he did not show me, or someone else, his wallet full of pictures of his little girl and his wife. That man lived and breathed for you two."

"Six months?" Danielle thinks for a moment. "The only time Daddy was away for that long was when he had to go on that cruise to the North Pole. Wait a minute, was that a lie too? So, then he was doing some kind of SEAL training?"

"Yes, Danielle it was a lie, but one he was ordered to tell. Jacob was by far my very best student who went through the program. He could have made one hell of a SEAL."

"Well, why didn't he become a SEAL then?"

Tommy stops and thinks about that one for a moment as he ponders a response, then says, "Your father chose the Coast Guard because he wanted to serve his country, but he wanted to do it by saving lives and protecting people. He did not want to be a full-time combat sailor. Now don't get me wrong, I'm a SEAL all the way, and we serve our country very well, but if your dad ever joined us, we would have ruined him."

"What do you mean?"

"Well, Jacob has deep emotions, and he cares for and values life so deeply that death has a profound effect on him. His sense of right and wrong and justice will always overshadow any obligation he might have to the military. He is a true hero in that he will do what he thinks is right no matter what anyone else tells him, or the consequences he gets. The things that we SEALs have to see and do would not have been right for him, and I think it would have been his undoing. Did he ever tell you about what happened on that boat off Honduras before you were born?"

"No, he didn't, but my mother told me when I was in college. She said it was the reason I got martial arts training almost my whole life."

Tommy nods knowingly and looks Danielle in the eye. "That was actually my suggestion. Jacob came to me about halfway through the training and spilled his guts about the whole incident and what it did to him. He told me every time he looked at is five-year-old, he would panic thinking that he might not be there to protect you. I suggested that he channel that energy positively and train you to protect yourself. From what I have heard, that worked out pretty well."

Danielle lights up. "So, you're the reason I had fifteen years of boot camp, huh? Thanks a lot, Captain."

Tommy puts both hands on his hips as he responds, "You're quite welcome young lady. Now go get some shuteye, we have a very big day tomorrow, and I expect my team to be one hundred percent when we hit the ground."

"Aye aye, Captain". Danielle says as she gives him a salute and a kiss on the cheek, then runs off to catch up with Chris. Tommy heads over to his Jeep Cherokee in the parking lot and says a silent prayer for Jacob, his wife, and mother and then mumbles under his breath, "If it takes my dying breath, I am going to reunite Jacob with that little girl."

At 5:00 a.m. Captain Maelstrom's security cutter docks at the Guatemalan port of Livingston. The six would-be rescuers leave the ship and meet up with some associates of Marnia's. As promised, Marnia's friends produce two modified late-model Toyota Land Cruisers, a full complement of assault rifles and small arms, two cases of military C4 explosives with radio/telephone activated detonators, tactical and emergency medical gear, and some extra clothing for their expected guests.

Marnia steps away to talk to one of the men who brought her supplies. "Did you get what I asked for?"

The man reaches into his pocket and pulls out a cell phone and hands it to her. "It is good in all of North, Central, and South America, up to forty hours charge with standard use. Here is a backup battery just in case."

She grabs the battery and puts it in her pocket. "Did you download the GPS app, and do we have unlimited data?"

The man rolls his eyes. "Of course, Captain. We are not that backwards down here. So, are the rumors true? Is the Hero of Cozumel really being held prisoner in Maximillian's private jail?"

Marnia is stunned by the question as she immediately calls Tommy over to her.

Tommy walks over and looks at Marnia and her companion. "What's up, Marnia?"

"I think you better talk to this man. He says there are rumors that the Hero of Cozumel is being held prisoner at Maximillian's prison."

Tommy looks at the Guatemalan soldier and says, "I think you better tell me where you heard that rumor, and how wide spread is it."

The man looks over to Marnia quizzically and receives a go-ahead nod from her and then looks back at Tommy. "We arrested a couple of guys in Livingston last week who were bragging in the holding cell that they learned how to do auto body repair in Max's prison, and that their work foreman looked a lot like Commander Jacob Edwards, but was wearing a beard and mustache. There are pictures all over of him down here and they swore it was the same man. No one took them seriously, but any talk about the Hero of Cozumel still gets a lot of mileage down here. I have seen pictures of his family on the internet and that is his father and daughter over there." He motions with his chin in Jim and Danielle's direction. "So, it doesn't take much to put two and two together."

Tommy takes all this in and looks very sternly at the soldier in front of him as he considers how to proceed. "What if I told you that Jacob Edwards, his wife, and mother, are all prisoners of Maximillian Manerez, and are indeed being held at that prison?"

"Amigo, I would say, how can we help? That bastard cabrón he killed on that ship had killed my father, who was a policeman in Livingston, and then later raped and killed my sister. He went to that same prison, but was let go in only four years, and then started terrorizing people all over again. No one was allowed to touch him because of Santiago and Maximillian."

Tommy looks over at the rest. "It looks like we have some allies down here. Marnia, see what aid you can arrange with these gentlemen. Everybody else, let's get loaded up and going. We have a five-hour drive and a good amount of work to do once we get there."

Marnia asks if all her personal contacts are on the new phone. The man says yes. She tells the both of them that she will call them later today and lets them know that the prison break is happening at 5:30 pm this evening.

While loading up the Toyotas, Danielle starts to notice some irregularities about their structure, not the least of which is that the side windows are at least an inch thick. "Grandpa, look how thick these windows are. When I lean on this door the skin doesn't even budge. This thing is like a tank."

Chris walks over and says, "It's a UATV, urban assault transport vehicle—used in situations of transporting VIP's through hostile urban areas. It's completely bullet proof up to fifty caliber, land mine explosive resistant, has a very powerful V10 engine, all-wheel drive, heck the tires are bullet proof too."

Tommy walks up and adds, "These are one of the reasons I agreed to take you two along in the first place. I am pretty good at hand-to-hand combat, but I wouldn't stand a chance against Jacob if I let anything happen to his little girl or his dad. Come on, let's mount up and go. Jim, Marnia, and Alex get into the first UATV, and Danielle, myself, and Chris in the second."

About two hours into their trip to the prison, Marnia's new phone rings. It's her assistant at the anti-cartel task force office. "Hello, Rachel. What's up?"

"Marnia, we just got a very unusual phone call from Jonathan Manerez in Guatemala. He says, and I quote, 'I need your help immediately. We have been holding Jacob, Mary, and Linda Edwards secretly here for three years. Now that you have arrested Boris, I believe my dad is going to kill them. We have a plan to escape this afternoon after our work detail. We have a boat waiting at the Pacific dock owned by my father and we are planning on sailing up to Los Angeles, we will need your protection once in Mexican waters. Please be ready for us.' That's the end of the quote. He also gave a cell phone number where you can reach him after 8:00 p.m. tonight. I texted it to you just now. Marnia, can we trust this guy? I know he helped us nail Santiago and all those gangs on the Guatemalan border but his dad, Maximillian, is our next target and Jonathan is his second-in-command."

Marnia knows she can trust Jonathan. "Jonathan Manerez is the biggest reason they call me The Cartel Crusher. You keep Colonel Ramirez off my back and get Captain Rohos ready to supply aid when I get back to him later." She uses the radio in the vehicle to contact Tommy and tell him about Jonathan's message. When she finishes with Tommy she closes her eyes and thanks God that Jonathan reached out to her first. But she still promises herself she's going to knock his head off when she sees him.

Tommy listens to Marnia very carefully and then responds, "Wow, I never really believed in serendipity, but in Jacob's case I'll make an exception. Don't try to contact Jonathan on the phone until he said to. We will proceed as planned; let's just make sure that when we make our move at the prison that he sees you."

While Jim is driving, Marnia and Alex begin to go over the details of how they are to blow up the extraction complex. Alex calls up an aerial map of the complex on his iPad and shows Marnia where he believes the best stress points are located on the building and where to put the charges. "I think that this is a major load wall here and it looks like if we set another powerful blast here we can achieve maximum damage. Also, it looks like they store all their cutting tool fuel here, so if we strategically place a blast here we can exploit the fuel tanks' exploding capacities and maximize the blast radius to encompass the entire facility."

It never ceases to amaze Marnia how well-educated these United States Coast Guard officers are. Marnia points out that the facility is going to be very well guarded, and in the early evening they won't have cover of night to maneuver unseen. Alex points out from the aerial map that the facility has a lot of windows in it and because of the hot climate most are open. So instead of trying to set the chargers by hand, they use a projectile to shoot the charges into the building and detonate them once they're in. Alex uses his thumb to point to the back of the vehicle as he says, "I noticed that we have a couple of goon guns in back. If I pack these C4s right, the projectile explosion won't ignite them, and the mobile detonators will work."

Marnia lets out a big whistle and puts her hand on Alex's shoulder, "I can see why Tommy wanted you along, nothing like an engineer who has been trained by a SEAL. Is that what got you into Tommy's program, your engineering prowess?" Alex is genuinely flattered by the compliment.

"You know, it was right after Cozumel that Commander Edwards called Tommy and recommended me for the training. Commander Edwards told me that surrounding the pirates at the aft of the Cruise ship and not having to fire a shot showed good strategic thinking. It just made sense to me to proceed methodically and cover all exits as we advanced. By the time we were seen by those guys, they had nowhere to go and being stranded by their escape yacht took most of the wind out of them anyway. Tommy's training augmented that type of thinking for me, and even though it was the hardest six months of my life, I am grateful the Commander got me in. Jacob's the best damn commanding officer I ever served under and I am sure glad I get to be a part of this team. I can't wait to see the look on his face when we all show up."

Marnia laughs and hits Alex in the shoulder, "I am with you one hundred percent on that one. Too bad we couldn't figure out how to record the whole thing, because I think Jacob is going to be one very surprised man." They both give each other a high five and proceed with their planning.

Jim drives and listens. No father has ever been prouder of a son, he thinks. To think that his little chunk of a boy he taught how to box in the back yard has earned such respect and loyalty from his peers brings tears to his eyes. He just keeps thinking, "Man I can't wait to get the rest of my family back."

Danielle drives as Tommy and Chris scrutinize the prison map to figure out where to gain unseen access to the compound. They both decide to go through some sewage ducts under the fence that open up in the sewage facility just behind the staff housing. After looking at all the walls and fences, they agree that it is too light out for them to scale them discreetly. Tommy tells Chris that there is some light scuba gear they can use, but they will have to rely on the smaller Glock 43 9mm handguns they brought because they could not keep the assault rifles dry. Chris laughs, "Well the Beretta 9mm and the Remington shotgun are practically all you ever let us 'Coasties' officers train with anyway, Captain."

Tommy always targeted the training to whatever outfit was there at the time. Most Coast Guard officers use a side arm in security situations. "Yes, and if I remember correctly, you got a ninety-eight percent accuracy score on your last test with that Berretta 9mm. A Glock 43 is considerably smaller to hold. Do you think you can adjust?" Chris notices that Danielle is intently listening to every word as they are driving so he says a little louder, "As a matter of fact, I have been to the range a few times with Danielle here and she really loves that Glock 43, so that is the weapon we have both used for target practice the last three times we went."

Tommy is intrigued. "So what kind of shot are you, Danielle?"

"Last time we went I outshot the cowboy over there," she says nodding at Chris with a giggle.

Tommy raises an eyebrow, "Really, that's interesting!"

Chris turns beet red and blurts, "That was like two days after the yacht incident where Natasha pushed me over a table, pistol whipped me, and tied me up. I was a little sore you know."

Tommy interjects, "That's the same Natasha that Danielle here had a life and death fight with and Danielle knocked her off the boat with a jumping side kick, right?"

Now Danielle feels bad for Chris. "Tommy, if it weren't for Chris, we would all be dead. He got out of that closet, found a

Taser and subdued Natasha with it, allowing all of us to gain our freedom and rescue the kids!"

Tommy is really enjoying this as he looks over at Chris. "I know, Danielle. I read the report, but something I found out while training this boy that you may or may not know is our young Lieutenant Rottanelli here is a pressure responder—the more pressure, the better he responds." Tommy puts his hand on Chris's shoulder and gives it a little shove, "Kid, she must really like you to stick up for you like that."

Danielle tells Tommy that Grandpa Jim is a fantastic shot with a shotgun.

Tommy just says, "I know."

Chris laughs and looks at Danielle's bewildered face in the review mirror and says, "When a man like Captain Williams says he read the report about the yacht, believe me, HE READ THE REPORT."

They make two fuel stops along the way on Highway CA9, and hit Quetzaltenango around 10:00 a.m. Tommy decides it's lunch time and tells the group that they probably won't get a chance to eat like this for a while, so they better fill up. He stays in the vehicle to look at everyone's plans and to cover last minute details. Satisfied that everything is in order, Tommy calls the group together one last time before they head to their different locations.

"It is going to take Chris and me about three hours to set up," Tommy says. "We'll be inside the prison near the staff quarters at 5:30 p.m. this evening. Alex and Marnia, I need that facility to go boom at 5:45 p.m. Alex, I like your idea to use the goon guns to cannon the charges into the building, but you have only two and your plan calls for three explosions. How are you placing and detonating the third?"

Alex smiles and slyly looks at Marnia and Jim. "Well sir, it just so happens that I have a champion skeet shooter right here with us." He pats Jim on the back. "Marnia tells me she has a pretty good throwing arm. Their target is the cutting torch fuel, so they don't have to be as precise. We have that new semi-automatic shotgun back there and Jim tells me he can hit anything within twenty-five yards. I think we're covered."

Tommy just grins from ear to ear. "And that's why this man is in command of one of the Coast Guard's finest ships. Good plan Captain."

Alex nods. "Thank you, Captain, means a lot coming from you, sir."

Tommy is about ready to dismiss the team, but Danielle stops him. "Hold on people, if there's one thing I have learned in all this, it's that I'm not doing a thing without asking God to bless and help us." She makes everyone hold hands and says a very simple but powerful prayer thanking God for protecting everyone involved and for getting everyone home safely. They all say, "Amen." Danielle then pulls out a 3x5 card from her pocket and reads the handwritten note. "Grandpa Roberto gave this to me right before we left. He wanted me to share it with you all at the right time and I think that time is now."

Joshua 1:9: Have not I commanded thee? Be strong and of a good courage; be not afraid, neither be thou dismayed: for the Lord thy God is with thee whithersoever thou goest.

They all say thank you and break off into their teams and head to different destinations around the prison complex.

Danielle, Tommy, and Chris head to a sewage junction station about a mile away from the prison. Tommy walks around back to the station's entrance, picks the dead bolt lock on the door, and goes in. He looks at the manhole and the automated pumping system inside. He pulls off the cover and sticks his head down in the hole, uses his flashlight to look around the tunnel, gets back up, and walks back out to the vehicle. Chris and Danielle are embracing in a light kiss when Tommy steps up. "Okay you two love birds, it's time to put our flint on. The good news is the tunnel is only half full on this end, so we might not have to do any swimming. The bad news is they don't have the greatest of facilities in this part of the world, so it is really rank down there. Chris, I still don't think we can take anything but the Glock 43s, but make sure you have extra clips. Danielle, it is pretty isolated here and I don't think anyone is going to show up, but hide the Land Cruiser over in that bushy area and just wait for Marnia and Alex's signal."

Tommy points to the road leading off to the side of them. "That road will take you straight up to the staff entrance of the prison. Let Jim lead with Alex and Marnia in front, and just follow him. If anything happens before then, you contact Alex and head his way. You have another Glock in the truck and a shotgun, which I know you know how to use, so stay safe and stay quiet. You ready Chris?"

"Yes sir, Captain, let's go."

They don their light scuba gear, radios, grab some extra clips, and head down the tunnel.

Danielle backs the big Toyota up and hides in the bushes next to the sewage pump stations as deep as she can and settles in for a three hour wait.

She thinks about her mom, dad, and grandmother. To think that the whole Edwards family will soon be back together again is making her heart go into overwhelming overdrive. As she muses about all the catching up they will do, a prison security Jeep pulls up to the pump house. Two armed guards get out and begin to inspect the now opened door. Danielle sees that they have not yet noticed the SUV she's in. Tommy and Chris are only a couple of minutes into their trek and she fears that they might be taken by surprise. She waits until the two security men disappear into the pump house and then eases herself out of the SUV. When she is sure the way is clear she grabs one of the Glock 43 9mm pistols in the center console and heads over to the pump house. As she approaches the door she hears the two men arguing inside. They are having a dispute on who is the one to go down in, and who gets to go back and report a possible prison break out attempt. Finally, the argument is solved by one pulling rank on the other. She hears one move the manhole cover over as the other turns the handle on the door. She steps back and waits for him to emerge.

As soon as the security man clears the pump house he is taken aback to see a female standing there a few feet in front of him. She flashes her pearly white teeth with her best smile, jumps straight up in the air, turns her head and shoulders to the left, spots her target, and whips her hip around catapulting her left heel into his left upper jawline just below his ear, knocking him out instantly. She lands like a cat in a crouched and ready position aiming the Glock 43 at the doorway. Within a second the other man comes running out while drawing his side arm. Before he can get it unholstered he sees his companion lying unconscious on the ground and that Danielle is already holding a gun on him. Whoever she is she just dispatched his fellow and has the drop on him, so he throws his weapon aside and raises both hands.

Danielle removes a pair of handcuffs from the unconscious man's utility belt then orders the other to take his out as well. She makes him drag his friend back into the pump house and handcuff him to a secure pipe in the middle of the floor. She then handcuffs the conscious man next to his friend on the same thick pipe. She searches them both and finds a couple of pocket knives and change. She stuffs their socks in their mouths and uses their belts to secure the sock gags in place.

Danielle is ready to go check on Chris and Tommy when they emerge from the manhole, having heard the commotion coming from the pump house. She fills them in on what happened. They are both flabbergasted at how professionally she handled the situation.

"I learned how to secure prisoners from some action adventure books I read," she says knowing that they are marveling over her work.

Tommy glances at Chris with a sideways wink and says, "She really is Jacob's daughter isn't she?"

"Yeah," Chris sighs, "tell me about it."

Tommy tells Danielle to leave the two prisoners secured in the pump house and lock the door. He and Chris will fasten the manhole cover from the inside. The pump house has no windows so he tells her even if they do get free we will all be long gone before they can get out. They all say their goodbyes again and the men head back down the tunnel. Danielle hides the security men's Jeep in the bushes and heads back to her SUV for the long wait. Fortunately for her, no one seemed to miss the guards, no one came looking for them, and their radio in their Jeep never made so much as a chirp. The rest of her wait was uneventful.

Chris and Tommy are glad that they are wearing airtight rubber suits over their clothing. Too bad they only have fifteen minutes of air in their scuba diving tanks instead of three hours. The stench is so awful; both are grimacing at each other. It's the foulest air Chris has ever breathed. Tommy says it ranks among his top five. Their progress is slow and arduous. Two times they swim under the foul muck, but at exactly 5:00 p.m. they are climbing the ladder into the pump station inside Maximillian's prison.

Tommy nailed it with his timing because he knew the guards that are usually stationed in this area would leave to be in position for the prisoners coming back from work detail at the auto recon center. This gave them time to take off their scuba gear. They have the good fortune of finding a big sink and a couple of hand towels where they can at least partially clean up. They throw their scuba gear back down into the sewage tunnel, check their equipment, and head for the door.

At 5:20 p.m. Tommy and Chris move out into the staff area, positioning themselves behind what they believe is Jacob and his family's living quarters. The plan is to get to Mary and Linda, secure them for safety, wait for Jacob to come in, and then wait for the distraction from Alex and Marnia. Chris positions himself below a window looking into the Edwards' kitchen. He peers in and spots three people. Two are setting up what looks like supper and the third is in a highchair playing with his sippy cup. "Both Mrs. Edwards are in there fixing supper, but there's a baby boy in there with them," Chris says rather astonished.

Tommy takes it all in quickly as he recalculates what is about to happen. "Well, I guess we are going to have to get a car seat for the little guy. If you see one, grab it. If you don't, ask the ladies."

Chris and Tommy hear commotion and cheering coming from out front of the cottage. Looking around the corner of the house out into the yard where the gate just opened, they see three guys attacking Jacob Edwards. Chris stands, draws his Glock and says, "That's Jacob. He needs our help."

Tommy reaches out and grabs Chris's shoulder and pulls him back down. "That's Jacob, alright, but he's not in any trouble. I have seen just about every move that guy knows and believe me he's not trying to hurt anyone, and they aren't trying to hurt him. It's a staged fight. He and Jonathan are making their move."

As Tommy and Chris watch the scene unfold, a black suburban pulls up and Jonathan Manerez gets out and runs into the cottage. Tommy and Chris look at each other and smile. Tommy says, "I think it is about time I met Mrs. Jim Edwards."

They both sneak around to the door and stealthily follow Jonathan into the cottage. But when they both enter three guns are pointed right at them. Linda takes a close look at the duo and shouts, "Oh my God, Christopher Rottanelli. Is that you?"

With both hands in the air and kind of an exasperated smile on his face Chris sighs. "Hello Mrs. Edwards, hello Mary, uh, we're here to rescue you."

Mary then lowers her gun, races over to Tommy, hugs him, and says, "Tommy Williams, thank God it's you." He steps back and puts both hands on her shoulders and says, "When I heard you were alive, I came as fast as I could."

Jonathan is astonished and relieved at the same time as he looks at the two commandos in front of him.

Tommy notices the look on Manerez's face and says, "Marnia thought you could use a hand."

Introductions are quickly made and the rescuers consult with Jonathan on his plan. Tommy likes it and gives his approval. "Let's get the three of them into the Suburban, and you go get Jacob. We will be covering your exit." Tommy lets them know that Jim and Danielle will be showing up very quickly, so he is going to have to explain a few things to them, but they can do that later when they are all out of there. Jonathan gets the girls and Roberto into the Suburban, which already has a baby seat in it, and drives the fifty yards across the lot to where Jacob is just about to fake punch one of the guys on the ground.

Extraction Facility

After Alex and Marnia finish setting up the goon guns, Marnia heads over with Jim to the second location where they will blow up the cutting torch fuel tanks. Alex uses his range binoculars to determine the exact settings on the goon guns. He checks his C4 charges to make sure they are properly packed and won't explode in the gun. Confident that everything is ready, he looks at his watch and sees it is 5:43 p.m. He gives Marnia a beep on her radio to let her know that he will fire in two minutes and sits and waits.

Marnia hears the beep and nods at Jim. She runs back to the bag, reaches down for the C4 cartridge and hears, "Stop, put your hands up and step away from that bag." She slowly stands and turns to discover she is being held at gunpoint by a prison guard. Jim is in position ten yards to her back behind a big bush and Marnia hopes this guy is not aware.

"What cartel do you work for?" the man asks in Spanish. Marnia shrugs her shoulders and feigns like she does not understand, all the while looking for an opportunity to present itself. Her opportunity arrives in the form of a huge explosion in the extraction facility, followed by another. The man impulsively looks toward the explosions giving Marnia all she needs to dive into the soft ground and summersault in the guard's direction. She lands right below the man's arms, catches his elbows in her palms, and catapults herself up with her legs pushing the rifle over the man's head. She simultaneously catches his chin with the top of her forehead and he nearly bites his tongue in two from the impact as she pulls the rifle from his hands and disarms him. She jams the butt end of the rifle into his neck just above his right jaw and below his ear knocking him out cold.

"Marnia, I'm ready. Where are you?" Jim yells through the bush.

"Coming," is all she says as she grabs the C4, runs over to Jim, and looks at him for a ready sign. He nods yes. She focuses on the big fuel tanks just inside the window about twenty yards in front of her, pulls back, and hurls the package into the window. At the same time Jim aims, fires, and then they both run back to Alex as the whole complex continues to blow to pieces. They grab the gear, get into the Toyota and head to Danielle's location.

Danielle sits ready in the Land Cruiser when she hears the explosions at 5:45 p.m. "Finally," she says as she picks up her radio ready to respond.

"Danielle" she hears Alex say, "we are on our way. Three minutes tops."

"I am here, ready to move in when you are."

Jim, Alex and Marnia pull up and situate behind the sewage pump house. Four truckloads of prison guards come around the corner immediately after and head toward the extraction facility. Marnia signals Danielle, Jim, and Alex, "That's our cue. Let's go." The two Toyota Land Cruisers head for the staff entrance of the prison.

*   *   *

Jonathan, Max, and Jacob, shocked by the explosions, find themselves standing in a circle facing each other. Max really wants to go check on his money with his men, but he knows he can't let Jacob escape. Still holding Jacob at gunpoint he says, "Jacob, this is where the story ends, I can't let you go."

Before Max pulls the trigger a lone figure steps out from behind the Suburban and like a charging bull catapults himself into Max's gun hand. Grasping the rifle he knocks it away from pointing at Jacob and down to the ground. He twists Max's hand in an excruciatingly painful wrist lock and uses his other arm as a bar to push Max face first into the ground. He finishes with a powerful karate chop to the back of the head knocking Max unconscious.

"Not today, Maxy boy, not today." Tommy glances at Jacob's bewildered face and says, "For crying out loud, Edwards, get that stupid look off your face, grab that gun, and give us a hand here—that's an order."

Instinct and training kick in as Jacob says, "Sir, yes sir, Captain Williams." He picks up the rifle Max intended to use to kill him.

Three of the guards try to turn the tides, but Chris slides in and pistol whips one in the back of the head dropping him to the ground. He uses the knife edge of his left hand to chop another one in the throat, then sidekicks his left knee and grabs the rifle out of his hand. He sees the guard to his right raise his rifle toward him, so he drops to one knee and fires two rounds from his Glock 43 9mm into the meaty part of the guard's left shoulder. The three prisoners loyal to Jonathan who were pretending to attack Jacob spring into action to restrain the three guards Chris just subdued.

Tommy looks at Chris and whistles, then nods toward Jacob and says, "Man, can I train them, huh?"

Jacob takes a closer look at Chris, gets a big smile and says, "Chris, is that you?"

Chris takes a deep breath and says, "Yes sir, Captain Williams asked for volunteers, so here I am. Good to see you Commander.'

"Good to see you too kid, and thanks."

Jacob says to Jonathan, "Where's my family?"

Before Jonathan can respond, Chris interjects. "They are in the Suburban where you need to be. We really need to get moving."

Even as he finishes the sentence the two Toyota Land Cruisers come roaring through the still-opened front gate.

The prisoners walking back from work detail subdue Max's remaining forces on that side of the prison as most of the rest of the guards are responding to the explosion. Both Danielle and Jim open their doors and stand up inside their vehicles hanging out the side to get a better look at Jacob.

Danielle shouts, "Daddy!" even as Jim shouts, "Son!"

Jacob is completely overwhelmed and sobs as his father and daughter hug and kiss him. The Suburban doors open up and Linda, Mary, and little Roberto excitedly run over to the group.

Jim and Danielle are in blissful hysterics to see everyone, but then a very awkward silence hangs over the scene when little Roberto is finally noticed. Mary clears her throat and responds, "He's one of the reasons we agreed to go on the trip to Australia in the first place. I was pregnant with him before we left, and an Australian doctor, one of the best in the world to help me have a baby, was there. We didn't want to tell anyone until we knew I could have him. Danielle, meet your little brother Roberto. Roberto, this is your sister and Grandpa Jim."

Jim and Danielle bend down and greet the little guy for the first time. He looks at both and says, "Mommy and Daddy and Grandma told me about you." He smiles and places his hand on Jim's and says, "you're Daddy's daddy." Then he wraps his arms around Danielle's neck and says, "Danielle, my sister." She starts to cry, lifts him up into her arms and kisses him on the cheek.

Then Jim and Linda's eyes meet. He pushes forward and grabs his wife, kisses her, and holds her with all his might, crying as they embrace.

Tommy's shrill whistle pierces the air and brings the festivities to a halt. "I think this is the most awesome Hallmark moment I have ever been a part of in my sorry excuse of a life, but we have to get moving people. The bad guys will be back any moment. Edwards family, you come with me. Danielle, you grab the baby seat in the Suburban. Alex, Marnia, Chris, you take the other Toyota. We're heading to the next location. I will signal you when we can stop and regroup."

Linda pulls back from her husband. "How rude. Who does he think he is talking to us like that?"

Jacob responds, "Mother. That is Captain Williams. Please be quiet and do what he says. He is trying to rescue us."

Before Linda can respond, Jim puts his arm back around his wife and gently ushers her to the escape vehicle. Danielle and Chris retrieve the car seat for Roberto and put it in the Land Cruiser.

Jonathan steps up to Tommy. "I am going with you. I have a boat waiting for us, and after all this, I definitely can't stay here." As he is talking, Marnia steps over grabs Jonathan's shoulder whips him around and slaps his face, "You bastard. You had him here the whole time and didn't tell me?"

Jonathan has been ready for this for a while. He puts his hand to his cheek and rubs the sore spot. "Marnia, my father would have killed them if you came rushing in here all half-cocked. I protected them for three years. Mary was pregnant, and in no condition to be on the run. Plus, Boris was still out there I could not take the chance this information leaked out."

They devolve into a heated argument in Spanish.

Tommy startles everyone when he fires two rounds from his Glock into a fence post across the yard. "You two can argue all you want in the Toyota. Now let's go."

Without pause, everyone loads up and leaves. The prisoners loyal to Jonathan tie up Max and the other guards they subdued and put them in the complex pump house. Danielle lets them know she tied up two guards in the other pump house and makes them promise to not leave them there to die. The hundred auto recon worker-prisoners scamper off to the surrounding woods. A few of them grab the abandoned Suburban and drive off.

Chapter Five

Rite of Passage

The Estate of James Harrington, North Jersey

Peter Rasmov was the only man in the world who had been personally trained to be a sniper by his uncle, The Chameleon. Boris was a very thorough but unforgiving teacher, and Peter had the scars both mentally and physically to prove it. Why uncle Boris did half the things he did was a mystery to the rest of the family, but no one could deny that it was Boris himself who catapulted the Rasmovs from being just one of the Russian Mafia families to emerge from the cold war era, to being a major worldwide crime syndicate on four continents. However, Peter's father, who was Boris's younger brother, was now only middle management as a crime boss.

Uncle Boris made sure that it was well known that his daughter Natasha was next in line to run the organization, which is why Peter is out here in the woods about seventy-five yards to the north of James Harrington's house, freezing in the late October East Coast chill. Natasha ordered the hit on James Harrington as soon as she found out that Danielle Edwards "Sebastion" used the marriage documents that they fraudulently forced her to sign, to take over all of the Rasmovs United States holdings, which included Harrington Enterprises. His orders were to eliminate Harrington and then search his home for any incriminating evidence that would link the Rasmovs to him, or jeopardize any of their clients on the East Coast.

Peter prefers the more modern sniper rifle as opposed to Boris's SV-98 old school Russian army issue. After a numbing wait, he finally sees Harrington moving about his kitchen and decides it's time to take this idiot out so he can get out of these cold woods and go search his warm house. He settles in with his Vinterez VKS silenced sniper rifle, centers his scope cross hairs on Harrington's temple, and squeezes the trigger. The only sound is a small puff of air and soft crack through the kitchen window, not unlike a pebble hitting a windshield on the highway at sixty-five miles an hour. The 9mm slug enters James's temple and he falls softly to the kitchen sink where he was standing, then slinks to the floor.

Harrington had been a recluse in his home for the last week since Danielle took over his company. She gave the authorities full access to the whole company, and right now it was saturated with FBI investigators, the IRS, and National security people. In other words, it was totally inaccessible to anyone else. Natasha did not think that even Harrington would be stupid enough to keep any incriminating evidence at the office, and was sure it all had to be at his estate in North Jersey.

Peter proceeds slowly to the home not knowing exactly what kind of security Harrington has in place, nor whether Harrington is being watched by the authorities. He has already made up his mind that at the first sign of trouble, he is out of there. It does not take long for trouble to show.

Still yet twenty yards to go to the front gate and sirens fill the air followed by flashing red and blue lights that fill the secluded woods where the estate sits. Two police cars pull up to the front of the house and four police officers get out and knock on the front door. When no one answers, two go around back and the other two force the front door open. By the time the officers reach the back deck, Peter is one hundred yards farther into the woods and is headed for his rented Ford Edge SUV parked along the New Jersey turnpike, two miles north of the Harrington estate.

Toting his gear, it takes Peter about eighteen minutes to get to the vehicle and drive off. He reaches down and presses the button to activate Siri on his iPhone and gives the command, "Call Natasha." The phone rings three times and Peter's cousin answers.

"I hope that you have some good news for me today, Peter," Natasha says, "I have not had much of that lately and would welcome the distraction." Peter takes a calming breath as he activates the Bluetooth loud speaker in his vehicle. "The good news is that James Harrington is dead. The bad news is two cop cars showed up as I was about to enter his home. I was not able to search his house for any money laundering records."

Natasha laughs. "It makes no difference, Peter. That fool kept all the records at his office in a safe in the floor under his desk. The FBI had the safe opened yesterday and have been arresting people all day today. That is probably why they showed up at his house when they did. You were fortunate to have killed him when you did. At least we don't have to worry about that pompous ass spilling his guts any more than what they already know. I have had five phone calls this morning from crime families up and down the East Coast threatening to go to war with us if we lose any more of their money."

"Well, I didn't stick around to see what the cops did" he explains, "I got the hell out of there. What do you want me to do now, Natasha?"

"Meet up with our people in Philadelphia and secure transportation to Falcon Lake on the Texas-Mexico border. Your next target is Will Harrington. For some reason, Maximillian is protecting him. Find out why, and eliminate Will as soon as possible."

"What about Maximillian? Should I consider him a target as well?"

"Absolutely not, especially if we want to avoid a war with those crime families I mentioned earlier. Max is the only one who can control them. My father never trusted Max, but he did respect him. You know as well as I that that is saying something. When and if Maximillian Manerez ever needs to be dealt with, it will be me who does it, of that I am sure."

"Okay, Natasha. I will let you know when I am at Falcon Lake, goodbye Cousin."

"Goodbye Peter, you have done well so far, keep it up."

Natasha disconnects and slouches back in her office chair in her apartment in Moscow. She thinks about how much her life has changed since her father's arrest five weeks ago by The Cartel Crusher, Captain Marnia Gonzalez of Mexico. She considers the American authorities were wise to let her have him. If the FBI would have arrested Boris, his many connections would have freed him very shortly after. Then, it would only take a very short time of him being out on the street before they would have been able to whisk him away to Russia never to be seen again. But sending him to a Mexican prison with the label of having tried to kill Jim and Danielle Edwards, the daughter and father of The Hero of Cozumel, and also being suspect of killing Jacob, his wife, and mother, made Boris public enemy number one in that part of the world.

On the surface, it looked like Natasha was finally going to fulfill her destiny and run the empire her father built. She had control of everything. Like her father she controlled all the legitimate business owners. She was now boss, CEO, and chairwoman of the board to all of Boris's underworld enterprises in Europe, Asia, and South America. Yuri had all the United States organizations in his name, which by some perverted twist of fate now put them in Danielle's control.

There was just one major problem. Natasha was running out of money. She had no rights to the United States holdings, and the FBI froze all those assets anyway, but her father had a financial provision that she was not aware of. All the profit, after it was cleaned and legitimized from all the businesses, was immediately sent to Boris's personal Swiss bank account, and therefore completely inaccessible to anyone but Boris.

She spent days trying to free up funds to handle the day-to-day operation of the legitimate holdings, but met nothing but roadblocks. She finally found the information needed to inquire at the Swiss Banking Institution, but was politely told that she is indeed the heir to all her father's holdings, and that those holdings will be released to her exactly six months after his death, which would have worked out perfectly if he had died five weeks ago when he was arrested. But as things stand now, the whole organization is going to collapse for lack of working funds in four and a half months.

Natasha laughs at her father's insight when she discovers that none of the companies will even consider holding back the profits from being deposited into Boris's account because if they do, a separate unknown entity will release damaging information to the proper authorities that will immediately shut down that company's operation.

Natasha picks up her iPhone and dials Peter again.

"Yes Natasha, was there something I missed?"

"No Peter, I need you to contact your father. We are going to put a team together and rescue Boris. Tell him to call me when he is ready to discuss the details."

On the Road to Ocotepeque, Honduras

About one hour into the drive, things start to settle down with Jonathan and Marnia. Chris is glad. Hearing people argue for extended periods of time is a little unsettling to him and Alex. Looking in the rearview mirror at them spoke volumes. There was definitely history there and not just the professional kind. Marnia finally said she forgives Jonathan and thanked him for keeping Jacob and his family alive. Jonathan made it very clear that he had nothing to do with, nor did he even know about the plane crash his father orchestrated until the Edwards showed up in the prison.

"After I helped you nail that dirt bag Santiago and his human trafficking operation, I lost my taste for the business altogether. I couldn't be my father's second and deal out the heartless cruelty he expected of me, killing and punishing people was not in me anymore. I was going to leave it all and join you in Mexico City like we planned, but then the Edwards showed up and I was torn. It was urgent for me to protect them right from the start or my father would have thrown them into a dungeon. I knew I could not tell you because you would have lost your mind and tried something foolish."

Marnia raises her eyebrows and starts to say something, but Jonathan puts his fingers to her lips. "Marnia, please just listen. Mary could not be moved any more. Dr. Chavez had to increase the concentration of her medicine because of the stress of being kidnapped and sedated with anesthetics. So, I settled in and protected them the very best I could. I made sure their living conditions were civilized. Mary had Roberto, and after he was a year old, Jacob and I started looking for opportunities for them to escape. But even if we eluded my father, we still had Boris to worry about. When my father told me Boris was in custody, I knew it was time to make a move, whether he was going to spare Jacob or not. I learned about Boris only two days ago when my father told me."

Marnia relaxes, takes Jonathan's hand in both of hers, and kisses it. "At least now I know why you didn't join me in Mexico

City. You are such a fool. I almost started to hunt you like I do a fugitive. Thank God I never found you back then, or Jacob would have lost his protector. After you reached out to me and offered to help with the Guatemalan border gangs I was hopeful, but I soon saw that something was putting a lot of pressure on you, now I know what."

Alex and Chris are relieved to see the couple decide not to kill each other and to just enjoy the quiet drive for a while. Not too unsurprising to them, within minutes Jonathan and Marnia are sound asleep in the back seat. Marnia's head gently rests on Jonathan's shoulder, and Jonathan holds her hand in his as they slumber.

Tommy decided to drive so the family could have some time enjoying their reunion. Danielle, her mother Mary, and Roberto are in the third-row seat. Jim and Linda have the middle seat, and Jacob is up front with Tommy. Jim and Linda are both lost in blissful silent cuddling. Danielle's reunion with her mother is very emotional. When she first got into the SUV and sat next to her with little Roberto on the other side, she became so overwhelmed with the situation that she laid her head on her mother's chest and cried for a good thirty minutes. Both Mary and Roberto caressed and consoled her until she got it out. She now sat silent enjoying their presence.

Tommy's happy that the family's happy. He turns his head toward Linda when he feels her hand on his shoulder. "I am sorry that I yelled at you back there, Captain Williams. It was so long since my husband held me that I did not want it to end. But I want to thank you for rescuing all of us. I see that my son looks up to you, and that is enough for me. You're in charge and I will do what you say from here on out."

Tommy has never been the sentimental type, but this family is really getting to him. He manages to choke out, "That's quite all right Mrs. Edwards, and please call me Tommy. I retired from active duty a few years back."

All of a sudden, Danielle bobs her head and says, "Daddy, I restored a 1967 Ford Mustang Fastback convertible this summer."

Jacob's eyes get as big as saucers as he swings around in his seat. "200, 289, or 390?"

Danielle gets a big ole grin and replies, "A 289ci, with 274 road slapping horses, small block, with a Holly 650 quad pumper, four on the floor, candy apple red, white top, and black leather interior."

Jacob, fully turned around in his seat, whistles, and says, "NICE!"

Jim sits up straight excitedly looking back and forth between the two. "I tried to buy it from the owner," he says, "but that dance guy from Russia gave him one hundred thousand dollars for it. Can you believe that?"

Jacob raises his right hand in the air and waves it at him. "Dad, you know those rich Russians and European types are American muscle car fanatics. Remember that dealer down in DC who you know? He would buy two or three classic muscle cars a year, put them on a boat, take them to Denmark, and sell them. The profit he made paid for the trip, transport, and covered his whole year."

Jim gives a big huff, "I know Jacob, but Danielle did such a nice job on that Mustang, I wanted to get it and keep it."

Danielle pipes in, "Well, I was thinking, the muscle car show is coming up in about five months. Why don't we go find something that the three of us can work on together? Maybe another Fastback, or how about a 'Cuda?"

"That's a great idea Danielle, when we get back to HQ, I'll start canvassing my sources. Sound good to you, son?"

Jacob smiles and puts his hand up for a group high five. "Hell yes!"

Linda sits quietly next to her husband with a very endearing smile on her face. She turns back and looks at Mary, "You know it's hard to believe, but I really have missed these all-about-car conversations between these three."

Mary wipes a tear from her eye, "Me, too."

"I want to play," little Roberto says, earnestly looking around.

The whole car erupts in laughter. Danielle smiles and puts her face down by Roberto's. "Well that's okay with me, little brother, because that's what we do in this family, play with cars. You're in."

Roberto reaches up, gives Danielle a high five, and starts to clap his hands together as he giggles with glee.

North of Mexico City, Twelve Hours Earlier

Boris sits in his private maximum security cell eating the meal that was just left for him. He smiles as he takes a bite of the rice dish in front of him using the plastic spoon. The assassination attempts on his life a few weeks ago were almost comical. At seventy years old he is still capable and still knows how to kill a man quickly and efficiently with whatever tools are present. Jamming the blunt end of a spoon into a man's throat and digging out his Adam's apple was one that worked very nicely in the prison cafeteria. He would have killed the other assassin as well if the prison guards had not stepped in and saved his miserable life. At least he now he had some privacy in this new facility.

In his next spoon of rice and beans there is a surprise—something different in the texture of the food in his mouth. He reaches in and pulls out a small piece of paper with tiny letters on it. Even before reading the message he knows who it is from. Only she would surmise that his eyesight is so good that he could read the message. Being one of the best snipers in the world has its perks. He holds the note up to the light.

YOU HAVE 8 HOURS—BE READY

When he was first arrested, he was nervous that Natasha would jump the gun and act emotionally. He knows how to control people who are greedy and power hungry. He is part of that group and understands perfectly what drives him to his ends. But people who do things for ideals, ethics, duty, and love, to Boris, are a lot more uncontrollable and certainly not to be trusted with any kind of authority in his organization. He made sure that Natasha was raised to believe the accumulation of wealth and power was the greatest of ideals. Those around you, the closest of friends and even family are of value only when they contribute to those ends.

It is a little over five weeks since his arrest, and Natasha is certainly feeling the burden of the lack of funds to keep operations flowing smoothly. He is pleased with her effort to take over and run things herself. That shows initiative and self-confidence. It also shows that he can control her perfectly. Had she acted earlier and tried to save him out of some misguided love for her father that would have ended her chance to succeed him. He probably either would have killed her or sent her to be with his sniveling sentimental brother who could never see beyond Moscow and the syndicate.

Boris sticks the message back in his mouth and swallows it. He finishes his meal and lies down on his cot. If they are going to be here in eight hours, the best preparation he can give himself is some rest; it's probably going to be a long night. With that thought, he closes his eyes and goes to sleep.

*   *   *

Peter is good at his job and he has not messed up an assignment in a very long time. But rescuing Uncle Boris is just not an assignment; it is more like a rite of passage. There will be either great reward or consequences coming his way at the end of this operation, and he is feeling the strain of it all.

He contacted his father to make arrangements for the very best men and women in the organization to be on hand for the operation. Peter had little difficulty sneaking into Mexico and easily managed to procure transport at Falcon Lake. His people met him on the other side. From there, it was about a six-hour drive to the hidden maximum security facility north of Mexico City where Boris was incarcerated. He figures it will be about eight hours before he is face-to-face with his uncle and teacher. Natasha assures him via a phone call that her father is ready and waiting for his arrival.

The five people who met Peter were all Europeans from Spain. For some reason, Natasha did not want any of Maximillian's people involved, so they brought the Spaniards in. The group consists of two mercenaries, an explosive expert, a computer expert, and a pilot. They are all fully briefed on the mission and use the six-hour drive in the Cadillac Escalade to go over the details.

The plan is simple—cut the power, blow the gate and guard facility, infiltrate the prison, jam all communications, kill anyone who gets in their way, meet up with their inside contact, find Boris, and leave. A fueled jet will be waiting for them at one of Boris's private hangars northwest of Mexico City. From there, they will fly to Moscow where Boris can assume control of his operations and start picking up the pieces of the disaster that happened in the United States last month. Of course, Peter knows this is all contingent on what his uncle will choose to do after they rescue him. Natasha made it very clear that once Boris is free, he is to be obeyed without question. Peter has no problem with that because he has been doing it his whole life.

In less than six hours, they pull up to Lake Endho north of the Mexico M40D de Cuota, which is the outer loop road around

Mexico City. The secret military prison where Boris is being held is on the northeast corner of the lake where the river feeds it. They pull into a parking area near Endho about two miles away from the facility. Peter gives last minute instructions, then he and the two mercenaries head straight for the facility. The computer technician and the explosive expert head farther south on the lake to the power junction stations that feed the facility. The pilot stays with the vehicle ready to respond for pickup when called.

Peter's team arrives at the facility and spends some time taking inventory of the guards and electronic surveillances. Peter pulls out the same sniper rifle he used to kill Harrington a couple of days ago and begins to sight in on the guards that are farthest away. The two mercenaries position themselves to strike the closest guards. When everyone is in place, they hunker down and wait for the other two to cut the power. It does not take long. They hear a slight popping sound coming from the south and in seconds the lights go out. By then, the explosive expert is already there, and under the temporary cover of darkness he runs up and sets his incendiary charges to cut open the gate. The charges take longer than a regular C4 charge, but are much quieter.

While the gate is being blown open, Peter uses his night vision scope, sights in his targets, and with silenced shots kills the two guards farthest away. The mercenaries rush in and use their tactical knives to subdue and kill the other guards closest to the gate. The computer expert tells Peter that the facility will be without power from the grid for a few hours, but the emergency generators will still keep the base fifty percent operational until then. Peter knows he has to get inside in order to cause any more damage to the base and its ability to retaliate, so he signals the five with him to proceed into the facility. Peter tells the others, "Once we breach the outside perimeter of the complex, we should be met by our contact who will direct us to our next locations."

They proceed to the nearest door, the northwest entrance to the facility. Inside, they meet a high-ranking guard who gives Peter the proper password, "Chameleon extraction." The guard tells Peter that the main security operations center is down the hall and to the right, and that Boris is being held two wings over to the left. Peter motions for the computer expert and one of the mercenaries to go to the security center while he follows the guard to Boris's holding cell.

The security guard helping Peter is a major in the Mexican army who has been on Boris's payroll for quite some time. His usual duties were at the customs office on the Mexican side of Brownsville where he assisted the Harrington's to pass the trucks loaded with cars through to Mexico. When they arrested Boris and Will Harrington fled into Mexico, the Major was able, with Maximillian's help, to look like one of the officers who helped Marnia crack the smuggling case. He requested that he be attached to Boris's security detail under the guise of attempting to extract more information from Boris, but his real job was to make sure that Boris was well taken care of and ready for a rescue attempt.

As he leads Peter and the others to Boris's cell, he can't help but wonder what his reward will be. Everyone who has done work for Boris has always been very well compensated, and he was definitely doing some nice work for him right now. On their way they meet up with two more security guards, but the Major orders them away to another area before Peter is forced to kill them.

Two heavily armed guards stand squarely in front of Boris's cell when they arrive. The Major gets one of Peter's side arms and proceeds to encounter the guards. As their superior officer, his presence makes the men stand and salute. He quickly kills them with two exceptionally well placed shots. He grabs the keys from one of the dead guards to unlock the door.

Boris knew the extraction crew was on its way when he saw the lights flicker and fail. Although the backup generators kicked in, his cell is not one of the locations receiving emergency power, so he stands there in the dark. He hears the two shots from a 9mm pistol, probably a Glock 19, and sees that someone is turning the key to his door. He does not expect the person on the other side to be an enemy, but he has not made it this far without being cautious. He stands to the side of the door with the food tray in his hand ready to jam it into a would-be assailant's throat. The cell door opens but no one enters. A familiar voice calls from the hall, "Uncle Boris, we are here. Are you ready?"

Boris smiles, because next to Natasha, Peter is the most competent person in his organization. "Come in Peter. Yes, I am ready."

Peter enters his uncle's cell with an illuminated flashlight. He knows better than to display any sentimentality, so he just gives Boris the report he is waiting for. "All communications and surveillance cameras are cut off for approximately twenty minutes. There is a clear path to the northwest exit of the facility and our transportation is five minutes away waiting for my signal. We have a jet waiting for us twenty minutes northwest of our location."

Boris raises his eyebrows as he gazes at his nephew.

"And yes," Peter continues, "I have your rifle in the Cadillac Escalade that will be picking us up."

"Peter, you have done well. Let us proceed."

Boris greets the Major and asks for his gun. He takes the Glock 19 from the Major's extended hand, turns it on him, and puts two rounds into his chest. He turns back around. "Peter, you know I prefer a heavier caliber for these types of operations. These 9mm guns make you use too much ammunition."

Peter is glad he already thought about that and reaches behind and pulls out a .45 caliber Glock 21 and hands it to his uncle along with an extra extended clip.

"Nice, Peter. I did train you well and I am not unsatisfied with your performance so far. Let's get out of here. I have many things to attend to."

Peter makes the call to the pilot driving the Escalade. On their way out of the facility they do not meet any more opposition. The two from the security room tell Peter that they were able to put the whole facility on emergency lock down, which should sufficiently impede the response time. The Escalade shows up less than two minutes after they walk out the gate where they entered earlier. Boris crawls into the front passenger seat next to the driver and the rest, including Peter, get in the back.

"Where is Natasha?" Boris asks as they drive away.

Peter expected this question. "She thought you would want a backup alternative. She is on the East Coast at Tampico with your yacht."

Boris lays his head back against the Corinthian leather seat headrest and takes a deep breath. "She was not wrong, Nephew. I must say, a very solid operation all the way around. You two are to be commended."

Peter knows better than to take advantage of any compliment his uncle will occasionally throw his way, but he is curious about something so he asks. "Uncle Boris, might I ask a question?"

Boris turns around and looks at his nephew. "If it is why I killed the major who helped us back there, three reasons. One, his death completely sealed his cover. No one will ever place him as one of my operatives. Two, he was also on Maximillian's payroll, and I did not want our friend down in Guatemala having too much information about my business. And three, he used that 9mm Glock to kill the two guards in front of my door, so killing him with that same gun makes everything look exactly as we want it to cover all tracks. Now, I have a few questions for you. What of the Harringtons, are they dead yet?"

Peter gulps. He really wanted Natasha to be the one to break this news, but he knows better than to hold anything back. "I was able to kill James Harrington at his estate in Northern New Jersey. After you were captured, he was able to work some kind of a deal out with Maximillian that made it look like it was an operation organized by his son William and Natasha. William fled to Mexico. Our sources have him hiding out in Maximillian's hacienda on Falcon Lake. James tried to keep his end of the operation going with the standard money laundering we set up through Harrington Enterprises. But he was sloppy, and now the FBI has the whole complex locked down."

Boris quizzically looks at his nephew. "They should not have been able to move that fast. Harrington controls only twenty percent of that business and the other ownership of the company is in a multifaceted layer of ghost corporations."

Peter had hoped that it would be Natasha who explained the next set of details to Boris. Seeing now that there was no option, he proceeded. "Uncle Boris, Jim Edwards was able to retrieve your briefcase off the yacht last month. He gave the wedding and corporate documents to his lawyer. Danielle…uh, Danielle Sebastion is now the controlling owner of Harrington Enterprises, Sebastion Auto Sales, and all of both companies' holdings. She opened up everything to the United States authorities and they are investigating and auditing everything you have on the Eastern Seaboard of the United States."

Boris is visibly shocked. His knuckles turn white from grasping the arm rests on both sides of the plush leather seat and his face is in a contorted rage as he mulls over the information. There is a dead air of silence in the Cadillac as it rolls down the road, each passenger, afraid to utter a word, terrified that Boris will turn on them to vent his rage.

Chapter Six

Split Decisions

Regroup, Off the Road in Guatemala

Tommy radios Alex in the other vehicle to stop for a regroup. They've been driving for about two hours and it's time to make some decisions. They find an area just off the road where they can park and have a little privacy.

He gets the whole group together in between the two vehicles. "I would say by now, Maximillian is free and looking for us."

Jonathan says he has a boat ready for us about three hours away on the West Coast ready to sail to Los Angeles.

I think that is a good option, but I also know that Alex's Coast Guard Security Cutter will be at dock in Honduras in eighteen hours. That is about a sixteen-hour drive. That security cutter is about the safest place any of us could hope to be on down in this part of the world, and I don't think Maxy boy is going to connect us to it just yet. But, I don't like putting all my eggs in one basket either. Jonathan, your father knows what resources are available to you down here, and I am thinking he probably is already having that boat of yours watched. That can work to our favor. Here's what I want to do. Linda, Mary, Roberto, and Danielle will go with Alex and Chris and meet up with the security cutter in Honduras. Jim, Jacob, Marnia, and Jonathan will come with me. We will go and secure that boat, or pursue other options as they present themselves. This will ensure that you guys make it to Alex's security cutter unimpeded.

Chris raises his hand. "Sir, don't you think that taking me and Captain Maelstrom along with you would be better. We three plus Marnia and Jonathan could handle Max's forces and provide the distraction the Edwards need. I don't like the idea of splitting up the Edwards family so fast. The Edwards could take one of the SUVs to Honduras and we could go with you. You trained Captain Maelstrom and me to handle this type of activity and we understand your style of command very well."

Jacob sternly looks at Chris and says, "I appreciate the sentiment kid, but I need to know my family is safe and sound and away from trouble. I'm the one Max wants, and I don't want Mary, Danielle, or especially little Roberto around when I have to deal with his forces. I've known Captain Williams longer than either of you and have been on several ops with him. We will get the job done, and I'll feel a lot better knowing you two are protecting my family."

Alex puts his hand on Chris's shoulder. "Chris, the Captain knows what he's doing and who he's doing it with."

Tommy laughs and points his chin over to Jacob. "Chris, I was always very impressed with your ability to voice your opinion, even under pressure, but believe me son, as Captain Maelstrom said, 'I know what I am doing, and who I am doing it with'. Frankly, I pity the poor sorry son-of-a-bitch who tries to get in mine and Jacob's way, and we all know what Marnia is capable of. Jonathan has the connections and resources. Plus, Jonathan's presence will keep his father's attention on us and off you. Jim, you have the soul of a warrior and your son wants you with us. That's good enough for me."

Linda speaks up. "Captain, I know I told you earlier that I will follow your orders, and I know that you need to show my son that his family, especially Mary, Roberto, and Danielle will be safe so he can have a clear mind. But, I just got my husband back and I will never leave him again. Where he goes I go, and that is final."

Jacob immediately stands up. "Mom, there is just not enough room in Alex and Chris's vehicle for one more person."

Linda simply says, "Well now there is, because where your father goes I go."

Tommy takes a deep breath looks at Jacob and Marnia. They both nod their heads in the affirmative. He looks over at Jim. "She is your wife, Jim. I will leave the decision up to you."

Jim stands up and holds his wife's hand, looks deeply in her eyes and says, "I have been married to this woman for over fifty years now. Any success I have had in life has been with her. When she was gone, part of me left with her. She's back and I will never leave her side again. She's coming."

Tommy looks at everyone, takes a deep breath and says, "Okay, it's decided. Alex you have command of your group. You and Chris keep them safe and get them to your boat. Marnia has some friends down here who want to help. We will give you their contact info. Use their assistance if you need it. Once you are back on the cutter, contact Chuck and the others. Tell them our plans. We will need their help I am sure of it."

Alex walks over to Jacob, shakes his hand and gives him a big hug. "I am sorry I did not get a chance to say how good it is to see you again, sir."

Jacob puts both hands on Alex's shoulders and gives him a light shake. "Knock the sir crap off, Alex, you out rank me now. Let's keep it on a first name basis, okay?"

Alex nods. "Sure, thing, Jacob. Hey, I think you need to talk to Chris. Something is eating him and I need him one hundred percent. Can you check it out?"

Jacob looks over at Chris who is periodically glancing in his direction. "Sure, no problem."

As they are breaking off. Jacob approaches Chris and puts his hand on his shoulder, "Kid, are we okay? You seem bothered?"

Chris takes a nervous inhale, looks over at Danielle, then back at Jacob. "Jacob, I never served with you in the military. Before I heard you were some big legend that everyone talked about, you were just this really cool guy that I worked for and who helped me get into the academy. But when I got in, everyone treated me different because I knew you. My superiors were always harder on me, and my friends always envied me. Then I got stationed at Brazos and I met Danielle again. Only now…"

Jacob puts on a big grin, winks at his daughter, puts his arm around Chris's shoulder, and rubs the top of his head with his knuckles. "Only now, you and Danielle are dating, and you're nervous about what I think. Am I right?"

Chris looks a little astonished. "How did you know I was dating Danielle? I have been worried sick about what you might think ever since Chuck and Marnia told us you were still alive. Before this summer, the last time I saw her she was your skinny little twelve-year-old daughter and I was a seventeen-year-old senior in high school. I guess what I'm trying to say is, are you okay with Danielle and I dating?"

By this time, both Danielle and Mary are standing right next to Jacob and while Danielle looks a little worried, Jacob and Mary are doing everything they can to hold back their laughter. Mary grabs Chris's hand. "Chris, of course Jacob approves, because I definitely do." She looks around at the whole group and continues. "Jonathan made sure that we were kept up to date on all of our families. We even heard about you two going on a horseback riding date."

Danielle is holding Roberto standing next to her mother. She shifts him to her other hip, and looks at her parents. "So, we were being spied on for the last three years?"

Jonathan interjects. "Not quite, but my father did ask his associates in South Texas and Pennsylvania to pay attention to you guys, mainly because of Boris. I was the one who insisted on any information that might help Jacob, Mary, and Linda feel more comfortable."

Jacob sees Tommy getting a little antsy. "Chris, Danielle is a big girl and I trust her to make up her own mind about this kind of stuff, but if you want my approval you have it." He then gets a sly smile on his face as he pats little Roberto's head. "The only one left in this family for you to win over is this little guy right here. We have been telling him about his sister since the day he was born. He might be a hard sell, I don't know."

Roberto smiles at his father and then folds his arms around Danielle's neck and lays his head on her shoulder. "Danielle is my sister."

Jacob gives his wife, daughter, and son a kiss goodbye. Mary and Linda both cry and hug one another. Jim hugs everybody and they all start to break away. Danielle stops them, but it's Tommy who says something. "I know exactly what you want and I am all for it. I have been on over fifty rescue operations, commanded over thirty of them myself. Not one of them has ever gone as smooth as the one I just commanded. This little girl insisted that we pray and ask God to bless our efforts and he sure did, so by all means, Danielle, go right ahead. Danielle has everyone hold hands but asks her mother to pray. Mary has a very powerful prayer for guidance, help, and protection. At the end they all say "amen" and break off into their separate groups. With the vehicles fully loaded, they drive away in opposite directions.

Alex's Group, On the Road to La Ceiba, Honduras

Alex had Chris get the contact information from Marnia for the two Guatemalan soldiers that helped them earlier. He had his own international cell phone that was very reliable and very secure. Being a Captain of a security cutter had its perks. First, he checked to see if his ship was on time and would be ready to receive them at port in La Ceiba, Honduras. Alex knew he had a sixteen-hour trip ahead of him, and he was bringing two women and a toddler across one of the most dangerous borders in the western world. That is why the next phone call was so crucial.

"Lester, this is Captain Alex Maelstrom of the United States Coast Guard. We met yesterday morning through our mutual friend Captain Marnia Gonzalez." There is a brief pause while Lester translates what was just said in his head. "Si, I remember you. Were you able to rescue the Hero of Cozumel?"

"Yes, as a matter of fact his whole family is down here now. We had to split up. I have his wife, daughter, and son. Jacob and his dad and mom are with Marnia and Captain Williams. We have a full day's drive in front of us to La Ceiba, Honduras. We're hoping you can help us out."

Again, there is a longer silence on the phone, but Lester does finally respond. "Capitan Maelstrom, most of the Guatemalan army is beholden to Maximillian, but there are a few of us who would die for Commander Edwards and his family. Give me a couple of hours to enlist some help and you can call me back. There is no return contact number for your call and I assume you do not want to give it out anyway."

Alex looks at his watch. "Okay, I will call you around midnight. We plan on driving through the night and resting sometime tomorrow." Alex then disconnects the line and looks over at Chris who is sitting in the front with him.

"I don't expect any problems," he says, "because I think Tommy is right. Maximillian is going to anticipate his son's move and go after them, but be ready just in case."

"Yes, sir, Captain." Chris says.

Alex grins. "Chris, let's keep it informal until we get back to my ship, sound good?"

"Uh, sure Captain, I mean Alex."

Around midnight, they pull into Guatemala City where they decide to refuel and take a break. Alex makes sure that everyone has their identification and passports Chuck Yeager gave them back in South Texas. No one counted on little Roberto, so they did not have as much as even a birth certificate. Jonathan assured them that it would not be an issue in Guatemala or Honduras. Alex felt the detail should be a part of his next discussion with Lester, the Guatemalan soldier who was going to help them.

"Chris, you go into the convenience store with the girls and Roberto. I am going to call our friends and discuss details."

Chris helps Mary and Danielle get Roberto out of the SUV and goes in to pay for fuel and let the girls freshen up. Everyone is very grateful that Mary speaks fluent Spanish because the clerk at the cash register doesn't speak any English and Chris was having a hard time explaining that he wanted fuel for the vehicle outside. As Mary explains and translates, Chris notices that the TV is on and that the news coverage is about the explosion and massive prison break at Maximillian's prison earlier that evening. When he motions for Mary to pay attention, they flash a picture of Mary and little Roberto on the screen. Danielle and Roberto come walking out of the restroom. She sees her mother and Chris both looking at the TV and takes a look herself. She immediately sees the picture of her mother and brother on the screen and decides it is time to get back to the SUV. Luckily, the clerk did not appear to be paying attention to the screen and tells Mary how much he needs for the gas that just got pumped. They pay quickly and leave.

Alex notices they're all hurrying. "What's up guys?"

Mary answers. "There is a news report on Guatemalan TV that Max's prison was attacked today by another cartel. It said that over one hundred prisoners escaped, and that some kidnapped a woman and her child who lived in staff housing. The picture they showed was of me and Roberto. The report said that authorities are looking for a Black Chevy Suburban with at least two or more men, an elderly Caucasian female, two-and-a-half-year-old boy, and his mother. They suspect that the Suburban is headed for Tilapa on the West Coast."

Alex takes this all in, sorts it out in his mathematical mind, and decides that everything is proceeding according to Tommy's plan.

"All we need to do is keep Mary and Roberto out of sight until we get to La Ceiba. That means we bring your food in the car and all bathroom breaks are on the side of the road. We probably don't have to get gas for another four hours, so Chris, you go back in and buy some more snacks for the trip and we will be off."

Chris is annoyed to have to admit to Alex that his Spanish is not that good yet and he needed Mary's help in the shop.

"Don't worry my Spanish is pretty good. I will go back with you," Danielle says.

Danielle and Chris walk back into the convenience store. Chris points to the grocery section to let the clerk know what they are doing. Danielle picks out some toddler appropriate snacks and some extra disposable diapers. Chris gets some more drinks and ready-made sandwiches. As they walk up to check out, Danielle's attention is immediately grabbed by the TV they saw the news report on earlier. This time, there is a late breaking report about another prison break in Mexico City. She stands there in front of the monitor for a while, stunned and speechless. Chris does not notice right away, having grabbed all the items from her for the clerk to ring up so he could pay.

"What's the matter, Danielle?"

Danielle turns to Chris with panic in her eyes. "Somebody broke Boris out of prison!"

Tommy's Group, One Hundred Miles East of Tilapa Port, Guatemala

Tommy drives away from Alex and Chris as they are getting the girls and little Roberto loaded up. When he looks over in the passenger seat at Jacob, he sees the deep concern and sadness in his favorite student's eyes. "They are in good hands. I trained both those men and they are some of the best I've worked with. They will get it done."

"I know, Captain, I'd trust my life to either one of them."

Tommy knows there's more, so he presses. "So, what's eating you kid?"

"It's just that, for like ten seconds, I got my life back and now we're split up again."

Jim reaches up from the middle seat behind Tommy and places his right hand on Jacob's shoulder, "Son, it's going to be okay. No one is ever splitting this family up again. Before you know it, we will all be at Roberto and Isabella's having some of his famous barbeque ribs for dinner. We will invite Tommy and the gang over. They'll think they entered paradise after eating those things."

Jim knows how to cheer his son up, always has. Jacob looks back at his dad as he grabs his hand and squeezes it. "Damn, Pop, I missed you. You always see the silver lining in things."

Marnia looks over at Jonathan in the third-row seat and wonders if she could ever have what the Edwards so obviously enjoy—family. Jonathan seems to understand her, and grabs her hand and kisses it tenderly. They are both caught up in the moment just staring at one another when Marnia sees Tommy looking through the rearview mirror and Jacob, Linda, and Jim turned around also looking at them. Jacob lets out a whistle and laughs. "So, Jonathan, you and Marnia, huh? You told me that you just heard of The Cartel Crusher. I didn't know you two were an item, pretty interesting."

Marnia gets a wicked grin on her face and then punches Jonathan in the shoulder, "Just heard of me, hey hombre?" Then she looks at Jacob. "If it weren't for this guy, I would not be The Cartel Crusher."

Tommy's curiosity is now piqued. "I thought you had to have some inside information on that one. That Santiago was one bad dude, just as powerful as Jonathan's dad, and a lot sicker—human trafficking, child prostitution, piracy, just to mention a few. It was the most successful Mexican law enforcement crime syndicate takedown of its kind in modern history. Two hundred and fifty arrests and convictions that culminated with the death of Anthony Santiago himself in a full out military type battle at his hideout near Falcon Lake. Cartel crushing is a very fit description of what you accomplished on that one, little girl. I just have one question."

"And what would that be, Tommy?"

Tommy grins sideways. "Are you the one who sent that sick, sorry son-of-a-bitch to the abyss?"

Jonathan smiles, looks at Marnia knowingly, and answers. "Let's just say that it was something we accomplished together and leave at that."

Tommy laughs. "Okay, I get it, works for me."

He looks over at Jacob and winks. "They really are an item."

Marnia smiles and says, "You know, Captain Williams, that information you gave me about your raid on the child slave training facility in the Florida Keys was a game changer." She looks at everyone in the vehicle, lets out a deep sigh and says, "Being The Cartel Crusher is the result of a phenomenal team effort. Friends and allies make all the difference."

Tommy's Group, Two Hours Later, Tilapa Dock

Tommy pulls up to the dock where Jonathan says the boat is waiting. It is the largest docking facility in Tilapa and their boat is on the very end. Tommy pulls over and parks in a spot just outside the gate. "Okay, we are going to have to leave the Land Cruiser here. Marnia, you should call your Guatemalan military friends and tell them where it is. These things are not cheap."

"I would guess about two hundred thousand worth of vehicle, huh Tommy?" Jim adds.

Tommy smiles at the old automotive guy. "Not quite, Jim. These have some features that I asked Marnia not to tell any of you about unless we needed them, closer to three hundred fifty thousand."

The six of them get out and gather around Tommy in back where he begins to divide equipment up for everyone. "I want everyone who knows how to operate a firearm to carry. Linda, have you ever shot a weapon before?"

Linda looks over at her husband who gets a big ole grin on his face. "She's pretty handy with a Taurus .357, but I think she'll do fine with that Glock 43 9mm you and Chris were using earlier."

Linda blushes a little and looks over at her husband as she kind of mumbles, "Jim that was almost fifty years ago, I have not touched that damn thing since."

Jacob looks at his mom and says, "Are you talking about dad's old duty pistol from when he was a sheriff's deputy in Story, Wyoming where I was born? How come you guys never tell me anything about those days?"

Jim chuckles a little, "I'll tell you what, son, when we get out of this, you and I will have a long talk and I will tell you what an Annie Oakley your mother was back then."

"Jim, you promised me our little boy doesn't need to know about all that."

"Linda, he is fifty years old and the Hero of Cozumel for crying out loud, I think he can handle it."

Linda grabs the Glock from Tommy with two extra clips puts them in her hand bag and starts walking away with Jonathan and Marnia. Tommy, Jacob, and Jim stand behind the vehicle for their equipment. Jacob and Tommy both choose Glock 21 .45 calibers, and a couple of assault rifles still in their cases. Jim looks over at the shotgun he used at the extraction facility to ignite the C4 charges and grabs it. "I have never fired a rifled semiautomatic shotgun like this before yesterday. Tommy, what is it called?"

Tommy grabs the weapon, pulls the clip out, and puts a drum cylinder in its place. "This is the Origin 12 semiautomatic with a thirty-round drum. A little heavy but you handled it pretty well before. What do you think?"

Jim grabs the shotgun with the accessory attached, puts it to his shoulder, tests the weight in his hands, and nods his head. "I like it. This one's for me."

Tommy starts to close up the Toyota, but Jim tells him he's got to find a restroom. "Okay, you take the keys, leave your equipment here. It looks like you can go over there in that café," Tommy points across the lot. "We'll head for the boat, see you there."

Jim thanks him, grabs the keys, and heads for the diner.

Jim knows that Marnia's contact in the Guatemalan military told her they would pick up their vehicle in a few hours. So when he returns to the Land Cruiser, he opens it, grabs his equipment, throws the keys under the seat, and locks the vehicle. He heads down the dock and notices it seems eerily deserted. A ton of boats are docked but no one is on or around any of them. The hairs on the back of his neck start to stand up as he nears the end of the dock. He turns the corner to the location of their waiting boat and is confronted by a scary scene.

Jim stops. He backs up with his shotgun raised. Tommy, Jacob, Linda, Marnia, and Jonathan are being held at gun point by a group of men in front of the boat. He can hear Jonathan arguing with one of them. "I am sorry Jonathan, but Maximillian said that if we find any of the Edwards who escaped, we are to kill them immediately. Max just found out that Boris broke out of jail last night and if he finds out about Jacob and his family, you know what that will mean." The man raises his rifle at Jacob. Jim's heart races at about two hundred beats per second as he looks for some way to distract everyone without further endangering his family.

On a yacht close to the group, Jim spots some propane grill canisters He chambers the first round into the Origen 12 shotgun, aims, and fires. The explosion is immediate, and the man pointing the rifle at Jacob momentarily recoils from the shock of the explosion. That's all that Jacob, Tommy, Marnia, and Jonathan needed to spring into action. They each lunge toward their nearest assailants, subdue, and disarm them in a matter of seconds. Jonathan attacks the leader that argued with him earlier. He grabs the man's assault rifle with his left hand and back hands him so hard with his right that he flies over some crates. But the group is barely able to get to cover before the rest of Max's men open fire.

The five of them are trapped behind a big wooden crate in the middle of the dock and have only the guns that they were able to grab in those few moments. Max's men had disarmed them earlier, so they are sorely outgunned, and outnumbered three to one.

The man that Jonathan almost knocked out calls out, "Jonathan, our orders are to only kill the Edwards. Your father wants you, Marnia, and the old U.S. Navy captain alive. You are outnumbered. Give up, please. I don't want to be the one who kills you, that would make things very bad for me as well."

Jonathan yells back. "Go to hell, cabrón."

Jim Edwards has never had any tolerance for those that threaten his family. When Boris and his people threatened to kill his granddaughter, Danielle, on the boat last month he was ready to face them all single-handedly, today is no different. He steps out from around the corner shotgun raised. With rage in his eyes and an unstoppable fire in his soul, he yells, "You bastards, stay the hell away from my wife and son." At that, he barrels forward, shooting everyone and everything that's not family or friend. In ten seconds, five of Max's men are down, which allows Jacob, Tommy, Marnia, and Jonathan to join the fight. Jim doesn't even notice. He just keeps advancing on the bastards who would take his family from him.

By the time he is close to the yacht, he's expended almost twenty rounds and five more men are down. The others flee and jump into the ocean yelling "*!Loco viejo blanco con una escopeta, corre por tus vidas!* — Crazy old white man with a shotgun, run for your lives!" Two of Max's men manage to get on Jonathan's yacht and pull away from the dock. Tommy and Jacob are covering the group of guys who just jumped into the water while Marnia and Jonathan run over to help steady Jim who looks a little bewildered after what he just did. Linda is still by the crate when she sees one of the men on the escaping yacht taking aim with his rifle at her husband. She reaches inside her purse for her Glock that Max's men missed when they disarmed the group earlier and takes aim at a jet ski fastened to the rear of the boat. She fires twice hitting the gas tank and causing an explosion that propels the man aiming the gun into the water.

Jim whips his head in the direction of the explosion and then back to his wife, "That's exactly what she did in Story, Wyoming, to that gang member's Harley, back in 1974."

Tommy beholds Jim and Linda and then slaps Jacob on the back. "Holy shit, kid, I feel like I just got my ass saved by John Wayne. Let's get the hell out of here before their buddies show up."

Another explosion catches their attention as Jonathan's yacht becomes engulfed in flames and begins to sink. The earlier jet ski explosion caused a fire on the yacht that spread to and ignited the ship's fuel tank. Jonathan looks around to everyone and says, "That was our ride. What do we do now?"

Tommy pulls out an extra set of keys to the Land Cruiser that they just left. "I guess we are driving in. Marnia, can you get us across the Mexican border?"

"That should not be a problem, Tommy."

Everyone grabs the remaining gear, rifles, and equipment off the dock and they head back to the vehicle. The sound of screeching tires announces the arrival of two more Jeep Wranglers with eight more of Max's men in them. Tommy gets everyone loaded, hops into the driver seat, and hits the button on the center console that makes a new console of controls fold forward from where the radio and climate control buttons were.

"I think it's time we used some of the extra features on this baby." The ping of bullets bouncing off their bullet proof vehicle fills the air as Tommy starts it up. They can feel a slight shift in the front end as two barrels extend out from under the front bumper. Tommy swings the Land Cruiser around and aims the vehicle at the two Jeeps.

"Fire!" he yells as he engages a button on the newly extended control panel. Two large streams of yellow fire shoot out and hit both Jeeps square in the face, torching them. The gun shots cease and Tommy returns the flame throwers to their stored position as he puts the vehicle in gear and heads out of the lot. The radio and climate controls rotate back into place as he pulls onto the highway leading to the Guatemalan-Mexican border.

"Marnia," Tommy calls out as he settles in for the long haul, "Contact someone in your government and find out what happened with Boris. This is a big game changer. Then call Alex and brief him as well."

Alex's Group, Approaching the Guatemalan-Honduran Border on Highway CA13

Alex was very alarmed with the news that Boris had escaped and he could not help but run through his mind all the possible consequences of that news. He began to mull over the information that Danielle and Chris told him about the prison break and the subsequent report they heard on the radio that Mary translated for them. A small transcontinental jet took off about twenty miles away from the military facility where Boris had been kept. It was tracked to a private airfield in Moscow, but Boris was not on board that flight when the Russian authorities searched it. Alex surmised that for some reason Boris chose to stay on this side of the world, probably to try and salvage what he could from his devastated organization on the East Coast of the United States. Up to this point, they were keeping it secret that Jacob and his family were alive and rescued from Maximillian's prison, but Alex started weighing the possible benefits of the that info being released now. Knowing that Max double crossed him might be the best way to distract Boris from finding Tommy and his crew going up the Pacific coast toward L.A. Alex reaches for his phone to call Marnia, but his is already ringing—from Marnia.

Alex and Marnia talk for about five minutes and exchange reports. When Marnia gets to the part about Jim saving them all at the dock, she and Alex put their speaker phones on so everyone can hear. Danielle yells out, "Way to go, Grandpa!"

Jim says back, "Thanks sweetie, but Grandma saved my life by blowing up a jet ski on the back of the boat. She did the same damn thing back in '74 to that biker's motorcycle when I was a sheriff deputy in Story, Wyoming—" Smack. "OUCH!" Jim yells, "why'd you hit me, Linda?"

Marnia and Alex cut the speakers as Jim and Linda sort out their little dispute. Marnia tells Alex that Tommy likes the idea of announcing Jacob, Mary, Linda, and Roberto's rescue, but not until they are on Alex's ship. Alex tells them if all goes well at the border, they should be there in three hours.

About fifteen miles away from San Pedro Sula, two Guatemalan army troop transport trucks pull up and surround Alex's vehicle. At first, Mary gets very nervous, but Alex looks in the rearview mirror and says, "That is Lester and our armed escort. They are going to make sure we can cross unhindered."

When they get to the border there are a few cars ahead of them at the check point and they have to stop and wait. Alex tells Chris to go talk to Lester about what to expect next. When he starts to get out, Danielle also moves to go with him. At first, he looks like he is going to object, but then Danielle brings up the language barrier and Chris begrudgingly concedes. They find Lester in the front vehicle. He tells them that they might have a problem because the Honduran border patrol probably won't let him escort them in a Guatemalan military vehicle.

"You should be okay, they have nothing over there that I know of that can harm the Land Cruiser you are driving. Once you cross, just keep driving until you get to La Ceiba. There, the United States Navy and Coast Guard can protect you." He hands them some documents that he says will make the border patrol allow them to cross.

Back at the Land Cruiser, Chris hands the documents over to Alex. "Lester says he does not know if they will be allowed to cross the border with us, but he says these papers guarantee we can get in."

As they approach the border check point, Lester's transport is first. When he pulls up, several Honduran soldiers run up and stand in front of his vehicle. He gets out and walks over to the one who looks like he is in charge, argues with him for a few minutes, throws up his hands, and walks back to Alex's window to talk.

"That is Capitan Torres. He is a bandit with a uniform. He is refusing to let any of us go no matter what kind of papers we have. I know what he wants. Do any of you have any American money?"

Tommy had already thought of this and had given Alex several thousand dollars in twenties, fifties, and hundreds. He pulls out five one hundred dollar bills and hands it to Lester.

"No," Lester says, "Just give me two fifties and five twenties. We do not want every bandito on the border coming after you if they think you're carrying a lot of cash."

Lester proceeds back over to Torres and hands him the money. Seconds later Lester gets very angry and starts yelling at Torres, but the Honduran soldiers step up and point their rifles at him, so he storms back to Alex's window.

"He says that the two hundred dollars will allow you to cross, but no other vehicles."

"Does he want more money, or is that final?"

Lester laughs, "Nothing is ever final down here when comes to money, hombre, but we don't want him to think you have a fortune in there either. Give me five more twenties and I will see what I can do." Lester walks up again, hands Torres the extra money, talks with him a little more, throws up his hands and walks back to Alex. He says I can lead you in with the Jeep, but the big truck, with most of my men is not allowed to cross."

Alex puts his hand to his chin as he weighs the information. "What do you think we should do, Lester? It sounds to me like he is setting us up for an ambush once we cross."

"Amigo, you are a sharp one because that is exactly what he is doing. I am pretty sure we can handle anything they throw us. You could not be more protected than you are in the Toyota. They don't have any tanks around here and that is about what it would take to disable this baby."

Alex is a little concerned for Lester and his men being in the open in that Jeep. Lester assures him that he is perfectly capable of taking care of himself, so they all agree that Lester will lead them in and the other transport will go back to its base.

As they drive through the checkpoint, Alex sees that Captain Torres and some of the other soldiers are trying hard to see into their vehicle. The windows are heavily tinted an no one can really see in but Alex wonders if that could work against them so he lowers the window on Danielle's side and Chris lowers his as well. Danielle waves and some of the soldiers actually wave back. As he is driving away, he sees that Torres is immediately on his cell phone with someone. He raises the window and looks back at Mary. "Sorry, but I want them to think that we are transporting a VIP and his wife, and not some type of money, gold, or arms."

For about thirty minutes, the drive is uneventful. Lester's men drive a full block ahead of the Land Cruiser to scout for trouble.

They begin driving up some winding roads that are denser with trees and foliage. Lester's men are up around a bend and out of sight when Alex's group hears an explosion. A couple of trees fall in front of their vehicle bringing them to an immediate stop. No one can be sure that Lester even heard the explosion or knows what is happening. A small truck full of several armed men pull up behind them and somebody yells in Spanish to get out. When no one complies, they start to shoot at the Toyota but the bullets bounce harmlessly off. One ricochets and hits one of the assailants in the head and kills him instantly. Chris reaches on his side and pulls out his .45 caliber Glock 21, chambers a round, and looks to Alex for direction.

"Just hold on; we are safe in here for now and Lester should be back any second."

As they are talking, little Roberto is caught up in all the excitement. He undoes his harness on his baby seat and crawls up the center console to look up front. As he does, his knee hits a semi-hidden button that causes the radio climate control panel to rotate away, revealing another panel with several buttons and switchers on it. Alex sees the new panel emerge and says to Chris, "Tommy briefed me on this. These are defense features built into this vehicle—a flame thrower, directional control, grenade launcher, turbo boost, road countermeasures."

Danielle can't contain her excitement, "Are you freaking kidding me? This is so cool."

Chris is intrigued as well, but much more concerned with the situation and asks Alex what they are going to do. Alex hands Chris his cell. "Call Lester and tell him what's going on, I am going to get us out of here."

He presses the button marked *road countermeasure*. They feel a slight shift in the rear end of the vehicle as a large metal tube extends out from the rear license plate bracket. They hear the whir of a compressor from underneath the vehicle as thick, hot tar filled with large sharp metal jacks shoots out at the truck behind them. The tar completely covers the truck and men begin to scream in pain as they are burned by the thick hot substance and struck by the pointed jacks. Alex pushes the button marked *grenade launcher* and a small LED monitor rises from the center console which shows the front view of the vehicle with a targeting crosshair in the middle, similar to a first-person shooter video game. Alex uses a little lever on the control panel to maneuver the crosshairs over to the large trees in the road and depresses the fire switch twice. Two big explosions rock the front of the vehicle as the middle part of the trees blow up in front of them.

Alex pushes and holds the *turbo boost* button and yells, "Everybody hold on!" He puts the vehicle in drive and stomps on the gas pedal.

The Land Cruiser lunges forward like a rocket and peels straight through the trees and debris on the road knocking all aside. As Alex fish tails around the corner, he hears Chris on the phone with Lester say, "We just broke through; we'll be there in thirty seconds."

Chris informs Alex, "Our escort is just around that next bend up there. Some more bandits have them pinned down and they are in a fire fight."

When Alex pulls around the corner, his group sees the Jeep to the side of the road with Lester and his men exchanging gunfire with a truck full of men, similar to the one that they just left covered in tar. Alex pulls up to Lester and cracks his window. "Be ready to move out when I attack these guys."

Lester gives a thumbs-up. Alex puts his finger on the flame thrower button as he positions the Toyota in front of the attacking bandit's truck. They see all sorts of pings and sparks fly as bullets strike all over the Land Cruiser and bounce off. He depresses the button. They hear and feel the thrower deploy as pipes extend from underneath the front bumper. Two yellow streams of fire shoot out and completely engulf the truck and everyone around it. He holds the button steady blasting everything in front until all the gunfire stops. Satisfied, he rolls his window down slightly and yells, "Let's go!" Lester's men all jump back in their Jeep and follow Alex.

Danielle leans forward and grabs Chris's shoulders and shakes him. "That was the coolest, scariest, most freaking awesome ride of my life." Little Roberto is screaming and clapping his hands with glee as Mary endeavors to settle him down. After about two miles down the road, Alex looks over at Chris, "We are going to need to refuel quickly. I used up almost all our gas back there in the flame throwing. Call Lester and ask if he knows where the closest station is."

Lester tells Chris that it is not for another thirty miles, but notes that he has five extra gallons of gas in his Jeep they can use. Alex asks if Lester thinks those were Maximillian's men. Chris relays the message. Lester says they are just border bandits that pay scum balls like Torres to inform them when something profitable comes their way. If he could have brought his other men, they would not have even tried to hijack the group.

The rest of the trip is pretty uneventful. They make it to La Ceiba in plenty of time to board Alex's ship. Alex's XO, Commander John Ferrell, is visibly relieved to have his commanding officer back and safe. "Sir, the vice president said he wants to hear from you as soon as you board. He also said he wants to see any of your guests as well. We have a video call set up and waiting for you right now."

Alex was expecting this and he motions for Mary, Danielle, Roberto, and Chris to come with him. Mary looks around and takes a deep breath. "Alex, this is a beautiful ship you have here. You must be so proud."

Alex takes a big gulp and turns around, "This was supposed to be Jacob's command. I just inherited it."

Mary steps up, puts her hand on Alex's cheek, and looks straight into his eyes. "You did no such thing. You earned every square inch of this boat. Jacob always said you were one of the very best officers with whom he ever had the privilege to serve. This is your command Alex. Don't ever forget that. Besides, we all owe you our lives now. You saved the Hero of Cozumel's family." She then looks over at Chris. "You both did."

Alex mumbles a thank you then briskly turns around and heads for the conference room to take that call. When no one is looking, he quickly wipes the tears that welled up in his eyes.

The five of them stand in front of the TV monitor and camera as the vice president of the United States and former commandant of the Coast Guard steps into the picture. "My God, Mary, it really is you."

Mary gasps a little, "Harry, I mean, Mr. Vice President, it is so good to see you again. Thank you for sending the cavalry."

Vice President Rogers takes a deep breath. "Mary, I hardly dared believe that you, Jacob, and Linda were really alive. Now that I see you, it is all coming together what we have been dealing with since Cozumel. I got a message from Tommy. He wants to reveal that you're alive and back in the states now that we have you. He thinks it will send Boris in another direction and keep him out of his and Jacobs's hair as they make their way home."

Mary looks over at Alex, "That was actually Alex's idea, and if anything can help my husband get back to me, let's do it."

The vice president looks over at Captain Maelstrom and Lieutenant Rottanelli, "You two make me proud to be a Coastie. Damn fine work, gentleman. Damn fine."

Alex and Chris stand a little straighter and say in unison. "Thank you, Mr. Vice President, sir."

"At ease, gentlemen. Now let's get Jacob's family home. I have you scheduled at Brazos in eight hours, so I will contact Captain Phillips at Corpus Christi and fill him in on all the details. Mary, the president is going to let me announce the news that you are alive this evening. Carry on, gentleman. Danielle, Roberto, God bless you and Godspeed to your father and grandparents. Thank God for people like Tommy Williams and Marnia Gonzalez. This whole thing is a fantastic miracle if you ask me."

Chapter Seven

Weighty Matters

Office of Captain Larry Phillips, Sector Corpus Christi, United States Coast Guard

The news that Boris broke out of prison in Mexico troubles Larry. After he saw the news report early that morning he called Chuck Yeager of the FBI and John Brown of the Texas Rangers as well. Chuck called back a few hours later. He'd heard that Tommy and the others were successful in breaking Jacob and his family out of Max's prison, but that they split up to protect them and give Alex's crew a better chance of getting to refuge as quickly as possible. Larry invited everyone to his office in Corpus Christi to talk about how they can support the Edwards getting back to the States.

Early that afternoon, on the heels of the two breakouts the day before, Captain Larry Phillips, Chuck Yeager, Major John Brown, Barbara, Roberto and Isabella meet in Larry's office at the Coast Guard sector command headquarters.

Chuck says to Barbara, "I'm sorry that we had to pull you out of your witness protection location, Barbara, but we need your advice. We know Boris broke out of jail last night, and we have not made it public knowledge that Jacob, Mary, and Linda, along with little Roberto, are alive and on the run."

Roberto and Isabella are very nervous about the news that their daughter is running and in grave danger with their new grandson they just learned about.

Barbara addresses them first. "I am not sure about letting Boris know of Jacob and his family being alive and on the run. He never trusted Maximillian, and news like this would cause a war between the two of them that no one wants to get in the middle of."

"So," Roberto asks the group, "am I to understand that after the prison break Tommy split them up and half went to the West Coast with Tommy, and the other half went with Alex and Chris to Honduras to meet up with Alex's ship?"

Captain Phillips answers, "That is true Roberto, and I just heard from Alex's XO that Alex, Chris, Danielle, Mary, and Roberto boarded about twenty minutes ago. Getting across the border was quite a challenge for them, they were ambushed by some bandits, but they were also aided by some Guatemalan soldiers. There is also no indication that Maximillian knows where they are, or even that the original group split up into two."

Roberto and Isabella breathe a sigh of relief knowing that their daughter and grandchildren are safe.

Larry continues, "Captain Maelstrom and Lieutenant Rottanelli really pulled off an amazing rescue run with the Edwards women and little Roberto. Alex is going to brief me here in an hour, but preliminary info indicates that it was life and death at the border of Guatemala and Honduras. I suspect we are in for quite a tale. The security cutter should dock at Brazos in about eight hours."

Isabella asks, "What about Jacob and Tommy's group? Do we know anything?"

Major John Brown answers, "We found out that there was a gunfight with Maximillian's men on the dock at Tilapa. Our sources report that a number of Max's men were wounded or killed, but there is no indication that there are any injuries on our side."

"Well," Chuck Yeager adds, "I imagine anyone going up against Tommy and Jacob better expect to get a very bloody nose in the process."

John looks around the room and laughs. "Actually, our sources tell me that Max's men got the hell beat out of them and were terrified by a crazy old *gringo* with a shotgun charging them and yelling 'you bastards stay the hell away from my wife and son.' They reported that a bunch of Max's men ran and jumped off the dock into the ocean trying to get away from him."

Chuck confirms the report and adds that they heard from Marnia that everyone was okay and they are headed to Mexico in the modified Land Cruiser. "That's where we think Boris still is, in Mexico," Chuck says, "We had some people track the jet that took off last night from an airfield just twenty miles from the prison he broke out of, and he was not on it when it landed in Moscow this afternoon."

Larry's phone rings. There is a bit of silence, then he says, "Yes, Mr. Vice President. I agree. I have everyone in my office right now and we were just discussing how to proceed. Of course, I will put you on speaker."

The vice president asks if everyone can hear him. The whole room responds, "yes".

"I just got off a video call with Mary, Danielle, and Roberto Edwards, along with Captain Maelstrom and Lieutenant Rottanelli," he says. Isabella gasps with joy to hear about her family that way. The vice president says, "Was that you, Isabella?"

Isabella clears her throat and says, "Yes Harry, it was me. I'm sorry. It's just so overwhelming to think that Mary is alive and had another baby." Isabella breaks into tears and puts her head on her husband's chest as he holds and comforts her.

"That's quite all right Isabella, I had a tough time not getting all choked up when I was talking to them. Captain Maelstrom and Tommy both think it is a good idea to reveal that Jacob, Mary, Linda, and little Roberto are alive, and in the states. We can't hold the ruse long that we have secured Jacob and Linda, but they both feel, and I agree, that by releasing this information, Boris will turn his attention to paying back Maximillian for double crossing him like that. Plus, if we can figure out where Max is, we can probably capture them both. The state department has been in contact with Mexico and all the South American countries involved, and none of them will stand in our way in arresting and extraditing either of them back to the states."

Major John Brown says, "Mr. Vice president, John Brown here, Texas Rangers, sir."

"Yes John, you have something?"

John moves closer to the speaker phone, "Well sir, my sources have Maximillian on the move toward his hacienda on Falcon Lake. We all know that Will Harrington is hiding out there, and we believe that Max wants something from him. We think that Boris entrusted something vital concerning his North and South American organization to the Harrington's. With James dead, it looks like Will is the only one privy to it, and that makes him Max's best bargaining chip with Boris."

"So, you think we should concentrate our efforts on the Falcon Lake property, Major?"

John takes his white cowboy hat off and brushes what's left of his hair back, puts it back on, and says, "Yes sir, I do. I have been hunting Max for a longtime sir, and I feel like this is his Achilles heel. That man ain't afraid of anything but Boris Rasmov. If he thinks he has something that will protect him from Boris, he will use it."

"Well, Governor Rich told me he can't remember the last time you were wrong about something, Major."

"Deputy Director Yeager?"

"Yes sir, Mr. Vice President." Chuck says leaning toward the speaker.

"Chuck, I'm going to contact your superiors. I want the FBI to give Major Brown and his team all the help he needs on this one."

Chuck nods at John and gives him a fist bump, then turns back to the speaker. "You got it, sir. I always wanted to work with the Texas Rangers."

The vice president clasps his hands together and rubs one against the other. "Okay John, you got point and command on this one. Everyone stay safe and pray we can get the rest of our people home and safe ASAP."

There is a unanimous "thank you, sir" as Larry disconnects the line and looks at everyone. "Well I guess I will see you all at Brazos in about seven hours."

Small Dock in Tampico Mexico

It pleased Natasha to hear that the operation was a smashing success and her father was once again at liberty to conduct business. Fifteen minutes earlier Peter contacted her and said they would be pulling up shortly. She knew Boris like none other and anticipated he would prefer and choose the backup plan to meet her and his yacht here in Tampico. Boris wisely sent the men from Spain back to Moscow in the jet where they would be transported back to Spain. Natasha's people informed her that the Russian authorities were there to look for Boris. She and her father knew that Russia would never extradite him back to Mexico, but that would just be one more expensive bribe he would have to pay to keep them out of his business. After he heard about what Danielle let the FBI do to his American holdings, he was in no mood to pay anyone anything.

A full-sized blue Lincoln Continental pulls around the corner and parks in the space adjacent to where Boris's yacht is docked. Natasha stands waiting on the sidewalk in front of the wooden dock as Peter gets out and walks around the car to open the passenger door for Boris. Boris gets out, stretches, and looks over at his daughter with almost a smile in his eyes. He sees that she has his beloved walking stick in her hands, one of his most treasured items. She ceremoniously hands it to him.

"It's good to see you, Father. I hope that the extraction met with your approval."

Boris looks at Natasha and then at Peter. "If only I could clone the two of you several times, we could rule the world. The extraction was exemplary. The news I received after, however, almost killed me and those I was with."

Confused, she glances at Peter for clarification.

Peter bows slightly. "I know you told me you wanted to explain what happened with Danielle and the American holdings, but Boris asked me about everything, so I was obligated to tell him."

Boris raises a hand before Natasha responds, "Peter simply followed my orders, which, I might add, he is very good at doing, not unlike you, my daughter. I am very angry at this outcome. I have had many hours to mull this over. I have concluded that there is no one to blame for this fiasco but myself."

Natasha and Peter are visibly shocked to the core that Boris would ever say such a thing to them. Unsure of what the proper response is, they stand speechless as they try to comprehend Boris's unprecedented admission of responsibility.

"Pull yourselves together," he says, "I have not lost my mind, but the truth of the matter is that I am not a young man anymore. My empire needs competent people to run it when I am gone. That will take intelligent, ruthless people who will do what it takes to succeed, who have minds to look at all the possibilities and choose dispassionately the most profitable course of action. In my organization, that is the both of you. Peter your lack of ambition used to bother me because I saw how capable you could be. I see now that your willingness to follow Natasha's lead is not a weakness, but an asset and strength."

Peter gazes intently at this man who has practically tortured him into being who he is today. He could never have an emotional attachment to him. Yet he sees the truth in what he is saying and simply responds, "Thank you, Uncle Boris."

Boris turns his attention to Natasha. "I hope you brought some other items for me."

Natasha, as is her manner, is well prepared and pulls out Boris's nickel-plated Walther PPK with and extra clip and concealment holster and hands them to him. "Your Cuban cigars are in a case in your room on your yacht, Father."

Boris actually smiles. "You, Natasha. I was never one hundred percent sure about you—until my recent incarceration. The fact that you waited to rescue me until you truly needed me was the convincing element. We must never let sentimentalities and emotions cloud our judgments. We have power and wealth because we serve it, not each other. That power will decide if we are worthy or not to keep enjoying its benefits, not we ourselves. I believe you both are coming to understand these things."

With that, Boris retrieves the Glock 21 Peter gave him earlier and hands it back to Peter. He turns and heads to his yacht, using his cane to negotiate the boarding plank. Half way up he turns and says, "Natasha, get me a secure line to my Swiss bank. I need to free up some capital for my European operations."

"Yes, Father," she says and begins to follow him up the gangplank.

Moments later Boris comfortably sits in his lavish room on the yacht that has served him so well over the years with a fresh lit cigar in one hand and his Swiss banker on the secure phone in his other. He is winding down the call to release working capital to some of his key European organizations. "I believe that five hundred million euros should be adequate. Please dispense it in the usual proportions and check with your accounting people to make sure that all my organizations are making their expected deposits on time and in acceptable amounts."

Boris writes a few figures down on a note pad as the banker talks. "You realize, sir, that all your United States holdings have been frozen by the FBI, and we have not received deposits for four weeks. You are on their ten most wanted list. Because of that, we must insist on hearing from you every three days from this point on. Failure to communicate will result in turning control of those funds over to your designated representative. With the death of Yuri Sebastion and James Harrington, the next in line is William Harrington, who is also on the FBI's most wanted list. If you become unreachable after three days, he will have an additional three days to contact us. If he fails, then control of those holdings will go first to your daughter, Natasha, and then second to your brother in Moscow. This is all according to the agreed upon directives that you laid out for your accounts with us and cannot be altered until you are in a situation where no one who is after you can legally apprehend you."

Boris pauses for a moment assimilating this information.

The banker continues, "Since the council had you execute Pedro Guerra three years ago, your position and contribution on the council has been exemplary. But with the events of the last month we have decided to put you on the same probation we were forced to put him on. I will be your only contact with the council until this matter is resolved and we feel that there is no threat of exposure. We have all profited from your contributions Boris, but exposure is unacceptable, you know that."

Unfazed by this information, Boris states, "That is exactly as I have designed this relationship to work. Thank you for your thoroughness. Good bye."

Boris presses a button on his desk phone, the bell rings, and he picks up the receiver. "Natasha, would you please join me in my room."

"I will be right there, Father."

A few seconds later she raps on his door and he tells her to come in.

"Natasha, please sit down."

Natasha takes a seat in front of Boris's desk and waits. "Natasha, you know that the way I control my organizations is by controlling the money that they make. My name is not on a single corporate ownership document in the world. That gives us the power of anonymity. I force all of these organizations, legitimate and criminal, to immediately deposit all revenue into my Swiss bank accounts. Then, as I see the need, I redistribute the funds as they require them. In the event of my death or incarceration, my bank has a set of protocols that are instituted to safeguard my money. I have just taken care of all my European organizations and there are no foreseeable concerns there. However, as you well know, my American concerns are in chaos. As of this moment, my biggest problem with my American concerns is Will Harrington. If something were to happen to me, he would have control of the funds in my Swiss account, just short of two billion dollars, which I find unacceptable."

Natasha leans forward in her chair. "As do I, Father, we must eliminate him immediately. Our sources have him at Maximillian's hacienda on Falcon Lake."

Boris mulls over what Natasha just said with his hand on his chin. "I too want Will Harrington dead as soon as possible. But what disturbs me even more is that Maximillian is harboring him. I am sure he ascertained that once the FBI closed down my Manheim operation, Will and his father became a major liability to me. Maximillian knows how I want him to handle my liabilities. So he would not interfere with my business unless he plans to use Will in some way to have leverage over me? It is a bold move, one I did not expect from Maximillian. He was always the most intelligent of the American cartel leaders and making an enemy of me cannot be considered very intelligent."

Peter pounds on the cabin door and busts in without being admitted. Boris is immediately on his feet rebuking Peter for the rude interruption. Peter raises his hand and says, "I'm sorry, Uncle Boris, Natasha, but this is an emergency, there is some catastrophic news."

Peter grabs the remote for the forty-two-inch curved high definition television in Boris's room and tunes into a United States news broadcast and sits down.

"Just wait a second," he says, "it's coming."

The anchor on the TV monitor reports that Vice President Rogers has just announced that Jacob Edwards, the Hero of Cozumel, as he is known in Mexico and South America, who was thought to have died almost three years ago in a plane crash in the Pacific Ocean, has been rescued, along with his wife, mother, and two-year-old son, from a maximum security prison owned by the infamous cartel leader Maximillian Manerez. He reports that Mary and Roberto Edwards are meeting with family and friends at Station Brazos, Texas after being transported from Honduras by Captain Alex Maelstrom's United States Coast Guard Security Cutter *The Protector*, but that Jacob and his mother, joined by his father, are still on the run somewhere in Mexico.

The anchor notes that the four Edwards were apparently rescued by the man shown on his screen. A picture of Captain Tommy Williams appears. The anchor continues his report and says that Captain Tommy Williams U.S. Navy Retired, is a former SEAL team commander and later trainer. For the last twenty years he has been the head of a joint military law enforcement operational training program to help other agencies receive training in SEAL tactics. Jacob Edwards was one of the first military officers to go through Captain Williams' program.

The anchor reveals that reports are not conclusive, but it is believed that Maximillian is responsible for the plane crash that was thought to have killed Jacob, his wife, and mother three years ago. It is believed that he abducted the Edwards from the plane before it took off and secretly brought them down to Guatemala where he has imprisoned them for the past thirty four months. The news anchor says that an anonymous state department source has revealed that the motive behind kidnapping Jacob and his family was to give Maximillian leverage to use against the infamous Russian crime syndicate head, Boris Rasmov, who also just recently escaped a Mexican military prison.

Peter clicks the TV off. He and Natasha nervously await a response from Boris. Boris sits deathly still for a few breaths. The tension that lingers in the cabin is so thick that Natasha and Peter can hardly breathe.

Boris rises slowly from his chair, reaches behind him, pulls out his Walther PPK, and unloads a clip into the TV. He puts the gun on the table in front of him and says to Peter, "Please clean this mess up. I'm going for a walk." He grabs his walking cane and departs.

An hour later Boris stands on the deck of his yacht leaning against the rail and staring out at the Gulf of Mexico. Natasha approaches and stands silently next to her father, also looking out to sea.

Without removing his gaze from the ocean, Boris says, "You were on that boat with me when we had Jim and Danielle right where we wanted them. But at the same time, the hit on Roberto and his family failed. Our operation in Manheim was completely compromised. Everyone was closing in on us and we were totally unaware. I have never been so foggy. It is almost like it wasn't me who went through that disaster. Never have I felt so inadequate. When I saw Danielle hanging on that pole, looking out at the children we sent away with Captain Bliss in the lifeboat, she prayed out loud to her god. The anger I felt towards her in that moment was the most intense I have ever felt in my life. She had to die right then and there. But that foolhardy old cowboy, Jim Edwards, intervened and stopped me. That's when everything turned against us."

Boris pauses and both continue to look out at the Gulf in silence.

"Natasha, I have killed countless men, women, and even children with guns, knives, and even my bare hands, and yet those two and their friends were so completely unstoppable to the both of us. Now I suddenly find that even my victory in finally killing Jacob was just an illusion." He pauses again for a brief moment. "Dealing death has made me what I am today and not just dealing it to my enemies, but dealing it for profit. Death has never let me down until now. I am at a loss, my daughter, as to how we should proceed?"

Natasha turns and faces her father with an expression somewhere between raw determination and terror. "Father, we must attack and kill all those who oppose us. Now is not the time to run, lick our wounds, and settle for what is left. We must show not only our enemies, but our allies as well, that crossing you is a death sentence. This is our only option. The news report says that Jacob is in Mexico somewhere. We already know where Will Harrington is, and if what you say is true about the access he could have to your Swiss accounts, then we know why Max is protecting him. Let us wipe the slate clean of all these annoyances and we will be free to rebuild our empire."

Boris takes his hand and places it on his daughter's shoulder as he says, "You are so much stronger than your mother, my brother, Yuri or any of the rest ever were. All save Peter. You are my heir, and he is your lieutenant. We will do as you say, and the death we serve will give us back more than we lost." With that, Boris turns to walk back to his cabin. Before he rounds the corner he looks back at Natasha. "We will leave for Falcon Lake and Maximillian's hacienda within the hour. Call every asset we have in Mexico and tell them to meet us there. I will brief them on the way by telephone."

Alex's Group, Station Brazos Texas, Same Evening

The Protector docks at Station Brazos Texas at 6:30 p.m. Alex is not surprised to see such a huge welcoming party for Mary and little Roberto Edwards. John Brown phoned Alex earlier to tell him that his people would keep the press back to let the family have some privacy. Danielle is with her mother and brother as they descend the gangplank onto the dock. Roberto and Isabella Garcia, along with two of their sons, are there to greet them. At first, the seven of them just stand and gaze at one another, not quite sure how to express the floodtides of emotions welled up within them. Finally, little Roberto pulls away from his mother and walks over to his grandfather. "Mommy says I have your name."

Roberto bends down with tears in his eyes as he clasps his grandson's hands. "That's right, I am Roberto, but you may call me 'Abuelo'."

Little Roberto looks into his grandfather's eyes. "Yes, you are my grandfather, mommy told me. I have two grandpas."

Mary rushes into her mother's arms and cries. "Momma, I have missed you so much." They all hug and kiss one another as Alex has their things brought down to them.

Roberto senior is holding his little grandson in one arm and hugging his daughter with the other. The group of seven makes their way to the parking lot in back of Brazos where they are able to meet up with Chuck Yeager, Captain Larry Phillips, Barbara, and Major John Brown. Mary gives Chuck and Larry big hugs and kisses. "You two have no idea how much Jacob and I missed you. Christmas is just not the same without you."

Major John Brown approaches Mary and removes his hat. "Mrs. Edwards, I don't know if you remember me, I am John Brown with the Texas Rangers. I just want you to know that Governor Rich and the whole state of Texas, along with the FBI, are doing everything in our power to get Jacob, his father, and his mother home as soon as possible."

Mary gets a wicked grin on her face. She meets her father's eyes and jerks her head toward Major Brown, asking her dad, "Cowboy John, the real life Lone Ranger, huh?"

Roberto smiles and nods yes to his daughter.

John puts his hand to his chin. "Am I missing something here?"

Mary just laughs, grabs his arm, and wraps hers around it and holds his hand. "You were quite a celebrity in my house growing up. Papa used to talk about Cowboy John, our own local Lone Ranger. He said you kept us all safe from the banditos and every time you would come through town, we would always try to get a peek at you. Sometimes, when you would come visit my mama and papa, my brother Rafael over there would try to sell tickets to his friends to come see the Lone Ranger."

Mary's two brothers, both local sheriff deputies, stand next to them and embarrassingly admit that it's true. Mary adds, "I am so grateful for all that all of you have done and are doing. I know that by God's grace, my family will be whole and together again. Thank you." She extends herself and kisses John on the cheek then sweeps little Roberto off his feet and heads for her parent's car. Danielle says she is catching a ride with Chris and will be there soon.

Danielle spins around to return to *The Protector* and is excited to meet up with Alyeks and Patti Yeshlton. She hasn't had a chance to see her old college roommate since she and her husband moved back to the States. She is especially thrilled to see the little baby bump in her friend's belly. Danielle and Patti give each other a little scream as they hug. "Oh my God, Patti! You're pregnant! That is so wonderful."

Patti starts to cry. "I am so sorry that I deserted you back at Temple without saying a thing. My parents were totally against me going to Russia with Alyeks, so I just ran away with him and a year later we were married. Can you ever forgive me?"

Danielle sighs. "You know, I was pretty mad at you but not for deserting me. I was mad because I thought you were throwing away your future on some wild fascination with a famous older man. But look at you! Married, pregnant, I could not be happier for the both of you."

Alyeks tells Danielle that the dance school he "inherited" from her is doing marvelously and that he has several universities interested in their two oldest dancers, Juan and Renea. Then he brings up Boris. "Do you think that he will be apprehended soon? I cannot go back to living like I did. His organization in Russia has made no attempts to contact me and I would like to think that the association is over."

Danielle puts her hand on Alyeks's shoulder and squeezes it as she tells him, "I don't know. All I can say is that now that they have proof of my mom, dad, and grandmother being alive after being imprisoned for almost three years, the whole United States government is after Maximillian and Boris. They are both right where they don't want to be, in the spotlight."

Alyeks nods and grabs Danielle's hand, "I hope I am not sounding unsympathetic to all you and your family have gone through. It is just that Patti and I see that we can be truly happy down here and want nothing to interfere with that. I know you understand."

"Of course I understand," she says, "and be careful."

Chris sees them on the dock and disembarks from *The Protector* to join the group. Danielle smiles and says, "Hey cowboy. If you're done with all that military debriefing stuff, I was wondering if you could give me a ride out to Grandpa and Nana's?"

"Sure, as long as we can stop and get a bite to eat. I'm starving."

Danielle introduces Chris to her former roommate Patti and the two couples stand and chat on the dock a little before Alyeks and Patti excuse themselves.

As Danielle and Chris are about to leave, Danielle feels a hand on her shoulder and turns to discover Barbara standing behind her. "I'm sorry to intrude, Danielle, but I feel like I never got the proper opportunity to tell you how sorry I am for being such a big part of all the tragedy your family has experienced these many years."

Danielle had dreaded the coming of this meeting for quite some time now. A flood of emotions rises in her. Her face hardens into a stern expression. She's ready to let Barbara have it, but the tear tracks in Barbara's eyes stop her. Suddenly, compassion flows within her and she feels great relief.

"You know Barbara, when I first found out how you were a plant to help Boris kill me and Grandpa, I was sure that the next time I saw you I would put you in the hospital. But now suddenly I find coming to my mind all the things that Marnia explained to me about what Boris did to you and your family, and all that you were made to suffer for him. It makes me sorrow for what you have been through. Grandpa explained to me how you and he came to a good working relationship at the business, and what you did to defy Boris and come clean with law enforcement was very brave and honorable. So I guess what I am trying to say is, yes, I forgive you, and I'm grateful for all that you are doing to help Chuck, Marnia, and Major Brown bring Boris to justice."

Sobbing, Barbara wipes her eyes with her arms, overwhelmed with great grief and regret for what she has done. Danielle is not sure if she has ever felt such compassion for another human being before but feels compelled to console the very person who aided and abetted in the planning of her death. As she reaches out and hugs Barbara a still small voice within urges her to simply remain silent and hold a strong and confident embrace. Danielle feels energized as she gives such loving compassion and forgiveness to this woman, like her hug is helping to heal this woman's life.

"Thank you, Danielle." Barbara says through her subsiding tears. "Nothing will give me more satisfaction than to see your family restored whole and Boris gone forever."

"Thank you," Danielle responds as they each step back.

"I need to go see Chuck Yeager," Barbara says, "so, good bye for now." Barbara leaves and Danielle gives her a little wave as she heads back to the parking lot.

Danielle returns to Chris who stood off out of earshot to give her and Barbara some privacy. Together they head for the nearest burger joint to avoid Chris dying of starvation.

Barbara turns the corner toward the parking lot and runs into Captain Larry Phillips.

"Hello, Barbara," he says, "I was just looking for you. Chuck said he had a strategy meeting with Major John Brown and asked if I could take you back to your hotel in Corpus Christi. I hope you don't mind." Larry is nervous and excited at the same time, a fact that does not go unnoticed by Barbara.

"Why thank you, Captain Phillips. That is so kind of you."

Larry is grinning ear to ear. "Please, Barbara, call me Larry. I don't know about you, but I am starving. Would you like to have dinner with me tonight?"

Now it's Barbara's turn to get nervous as she realizes she has not been on a genuine date with a man since before she met Boris. "Yes, Larry, that would be wonderful."

Larry is very excited now and points to the direction of his car. As they cross the parking lot, Barbara reaches out to grab Larry's arm to have him escort her the rest of the way.

Next Day, Roberto Garcia's Home

At 5:00 a.m. the next morning, Isabella wakes to find that her Roberto never made it to bed the night before. She heads to the one place she knows her husband will probably be. In the back of their house is a very large, old coat closet that she and Roberto fixed up to be a little prayer room and quiet Bible study room for the both of them. A big easy chair, small desk, and book shelf outfit the little room with just enough spare room for a person to turn about and use the space. Oftentimes when one of them feels the need to pray or study intensely for a time, they isolate themselves in this peaceful, secluded place to get quiet with their heavenly Father and think things through. She and Roberto found that they both used the room quite frequently in the last few months. She lightly taps on the door and opens it to find Roberto wide awake with a Bible in his lap and a kind of fire in his eye that usually shows up when he is teaching at their fellowship.

"What has God been teaching you tonight, *mi esposo?*"

Roberto is so pleased that his wife showed up at that precise moment. "I have been up studying this one verse of scripture all night, Isabella. *I John 4:4: Ye are of God little children and have overcome them. Because greater is he that is in you, than he that is in the world.* I feel that I need to know and see this deeper than I do. I have looked at the life of David, and Jesus, and how they confronted and overcame evil men by the power of God in their lives, and I feel deep inside that I will be called upon to do the same shortly."

Roberto pauses, sips his coffee, and takes his reading glasses off. "Isabella," he says holding her eyes with a steadfast gaze, "some of the finest law enforcement and military people I have ever known are helping us right now, but that will not be enough for what is coming. This evil that has been attacking the Edwards family and our family is being channeled through Boris, he's the conduit. We need to make sure that we don't just rely on the strength of our flesh to stop it and to stop him from causing anymore heartache and despair. The battle is the Lord's, and He will fight for us if we let Him."

Isabella sees the truth in her husband's words as and says, "Darling, Danielle and Chris know that it is God who brought us this far, and I think Jim does as well. We will have our family back and whole when this is over. Of that I am sure." She leans down and kisses her husband on the forehead.

"Breakfast will be ready at nine," she says, "so try to get a little rest before then, okay?"

He promises her that he will, stands, stretches, turns off his reading lamp, and heads for their bedroom.

Chapter Eight

Just a Tease

Tommy's Group, Mexico City, Same Morning

The road markers indicate to Jacob, who is now driving, that they will be in Mexico City within an hour. He offered to drive late last night and Tommy, running on thirty-six hours with little to no rest, conceded. Within minutes Tommy was sound asleep and just now seems to be stirring a bit. Jacob gives his dad a shove in the seat next to him to wake him up. Jim shoots straight up from leaning his head on the door. "Wow, son. Did I doze again? I'm sorry. How long have you been driving alone?"

Jacob laughs. "You dozed off for the fourth time around midnight and I just let you sleep. We're about an hour outside the city. It's six right now."

Jim raises both arms over his head gives a big old yawn with his stretch. He reaches over and pats his son on the left shoulder. "God, it is good to have you and your mother back, son. It has been so hard without you. I don't know what I would've done if I did not have Danielle to talk to."

Jacob looks over at his father with a quizzical smile. "You handled her moving down to South Texas pretty well. When Jonathan told us, I didn't know how you would react."

Jim thinks about it for a moment and then responds, "I was pretty upset at first, but after I thought about it for a while, something just kept telling me it was the right thing for all of us. Now that I know what that bastard Boris was up to, I am convinced she did the very best thing."

Jacob tells his father that he, Mary, and his mother came to the same conclusion when Jonathan told them. Jim looks over his shoulder to the farthest back seat where Linda and Marnia are sleeping, and then at Jonathan and Tommy in the middle row, and says "You know, it's wild how we have had such fantastic people just come out of the woodwork to help us. I am really starting to believe that Mary's dad is right about God, the Bible, praying, and stuff."

Tommy's eyes pop open. "Boy, you're right on that one, Jim. I have never been in an operation like this. We've literally had no causalities whatsoever, not even light wounds. I agreed to bring you and Danielle along mostly because of your EMT training. So far, we haven't even needed that."

Marnia lifts her head. "Yes, but I'm glad we made the others guys suffer their share, that's for sure."

Both Linda and Jonathan groan and tell everyone to be quiet, it's too early for a group discussion.

An hour later Jacob navigates the streets of downtown Mexico City and Marnia suggests that they get breakfast before they head to her headquarters. She also wants to call her assistant, Rachel, and make sure that everything is ready for their arrival. While at an outdoor restaurant, she walks away from the group and calls her office number. The phone rings twice and someone hangs up the other end. Just as she hits redial, Marnia gets a text from Rachel's cell phone that says: *Call me in fifteen minutes.*

Marnia darts back to the restaurant table where everyone sits and tells them about the suspicious text. She shakes her head and sighs. "That means it's not safe to call the task force line. We better get out of the public eye fast, something's up."

The group jumps to action. Tommy pays the bill while they reconvene at the Land Cruiser. Tommy takes the driver's seat while the rest board. "Okay, Marnia," he says, "where to?"

Marnia's first military assignment in Mexico City led to her meeting a very interesting contact who consequently also became one of her best allies. She directs Tommy to the side of town with all the brothels. She guides him to a big, old, but posh looking hotel with an underground parking garage. He pulls in and parks and Marnia tells everyone to wait while she checks things out and she heads off for the underground entrance. She raps three times on a service entrance door and a rather large, burly Mexican man opens the door, recognizes her, and lets her in.

"Pedro, where is your boss. I need to speak with her right now." He tells her to wait in the hallway and goes into another room.

Marnia pulls out her cell phone and calls Rachel. She picks up frantically. "Oh my God, Marnia I can't believe what is going on around here. Colonel Ramirez just put out a shoot-on-sight order for you. He told the press earlier today that you have been an implant from Maximillian's Cartel, and that you have used your military and government connections to commit treason for him. The word is that you are fleeing to the United States with Jonathan Manerez to trade Mexican national security secrets for sanctuary."

Marnia processes the alarming news for a few seconds. She knows the source. Only one man could have the power to pull this off. "Rachel, this is Boris's doing. He stole secrets on almost everyone in our government from my father years ago. When I arrested him I had to keep him from contacting any of his assets. But now that he is free, he has activated this deception. He's after the Edwards, and especially Jacob. I am sure he is trying to lure Maximillian out into the open so he can kill him as well. Does Ramirez know that I am in the city yet?"

Rachel tells Marnia that she doesn't think so, but that they should stay hidden until they can figure a safe way to get out. Marnia tells Rachel to erase from her phone any record of contact with her in the last seventy-two hours and then to go back to work and lay low until she can communicate with her safely, and disconnects.

Pedro comes back out with a very tall and beautiful middle-aged black woman named Rosemary Sargent. She is an old comrade of Marnia's from her first days in the city. She runs a legal brothel through the hotel, but in a very unorthodox way, even for Mexico City. She only hires girls who come to her for work, and only if they are over eighteen and agree to stay off drugs. She provides paid-for health care and regular checks. She abhors the exploitation and sex trafficking of children and helped Marnia take down many child prostitution and human trafficking rings in the city. Marnia knew she was a madam, but loved her anyway and left her alone. Rosemary was always there for her when she needed help.

"Marnia, my little alley cat, what kind of trouble have you gotten yourself into this time that Auntie Rosemary needs to help you with?"

Marnia laughs at her old friend and gives her a big hug and kiss on the cheek. "Well, I'm here to close you down, madam, we can't have this kind of thing going on in this upstanding neighborhood."

Rosemary laughs at the old joke and says, "Actually, I know why you're here because your boss just called me and threatened to do just that if I don't turn you in when you show up."

Marnia looks at her friend quizzically. "Which we both know you won't because you are my friend, si?"

"Honey, I watch the news. You have the Hero of Cozumel out there with his dad and mom, and some sexy old man who I am dying to meet, plus *lover boy* I hear."

Warmth fills Marnia's face as she blushes at the mention of Jonathan.

Rosemary gives her a big hug again and says, "Girl, you go out there and get those people inside, we are going to set you up. But you make sure that Commander Edwards knows how much I helped you get all those creep child prostitute rings and human traffickers off the streets. I'm too damned old to be flying out some window."

Marnia returns to the parking garage laughing at what Rosemary just said, but realizing she was smart, because it could become an issue. Jonathan told her about what Jacob did to Frankie in prison a few years ago, and all he did was just brag about molesting girls. She knew that Jacob did not approve of any kind of exploitation of women, and would not hesitate to violently impose his beliefs in the situation. She gets into the Land Cruiser and closes the door.

"Jacob, I need to let you know that we are going to be hiding out in a brothel."

Jonathan has been nervous since they got here. "Marnia, I don't think that is a very good idea."

The whole group is tense as Jacob sits in the passenger seat next to Tommy and stares out the front window unwilling to look at the rest of them.

"Are there any children in there?"

Marnia lets out a big puff. "No, Jacob. All the girls are adults and were hired of their own free will. My friend Rosemary is the one I wrote to you about when I first started in Mexico City. She was a crucial ally and helped me clean up a lot of child prostitute rings and human trafficking here. She hates the exploitation of children as much as you. She's good people."

Jacob sits quietly contemplating what he is hearing. After a brief silence he says, "I just don't like being around that stuff.

I have no tolerance for the kind of animals who associate in these circles. Ever since that yacht off Honduras where Chuck and I found that family slaughtered and then that little girl dying in my arms, it's like this demon out there that mocks me, and God knows who that madman is hurting now. Sometimes it really eats at me."

Finally the moment of truth had come. With an incredible intensity hanging in the air, Jonathan, who has befriended this man so deeply over the past few years, says in a tense and nervous voice, "Jacob, you killed that demon thirteen years ago off the coast of Cozumel, and you put another of his crew out of action three years ago."

Jacob whips his head around and stars at Jonathan with fierce intensity. "What are you talking about? How could you know anything about all this?"

Marnia cuts in. "You never told him, did you?"

"My Father told me if I ever told Jacob about Dominik he would kill the Edwards, all of them. I didn't test him."

"Dominik Thrace," Tommy interjects, "Isn't that the name of the Jamaican that Jacob threw off that cruise ship?"

Jonathan nods yes.

"He was also known as '*Comodor infantile de diablo*—the devil child eater," Marnia adds. "He was a serial child molester and human trafficking lord in Central America." She hesitates to go on, but knows she must. "He was also the man who boarded that yacht off the coast of Honduras and mutilated that family and ravaged that little girl who died in Jacob's arms. That monster would have done the same thing to me if Jacob hadn't stopped him."

The tension seems to subside just a little as she directs her gaze to Jacob's swimming eyes. "Haven't you ever wondered why we call you the Hero of Cozumel down here? Dominik Thrace was protected by the Manerez and Santiago Cartels in Central America and was basically free to rape and pillage at his leisure. When you killed him in Cozumel, you freed a lot of people from fear and even slavery."

Jacob turns to Jonathan. "So, Frankie was a part of the crew on that yacht? Who was the other guy?"

Jonathan shrugs and glances at Marnia for help, but she shrugs too and then looks back at Jacob.

Jonathan continues, "I don't know his name. He was a younger Russian guy who Boris put on Dominik's crew. That's all I know. As far as Dominik goes, Santiago and my father basically gave that animal to Boris because they could not control him and Boris assured them that he could."

Jacob's lips curl down for a second as he turns back to Marnia. "How come you never told me all this, Marnia?"

Grabbing and holding his shoulder, Marnia says, "I never knew all the details until I met Jonathan. I wrote you a letter and was going to send it the same day your plane crashed and we thought you all died. I still have the letter in my apartment. I will give it to you sometime."

Jacob spins back around in his seat and sits there staring at the wall out the windshield.

Tommy puts his hand on Jacobs shoulder. "You okay, kid?"

Jacob sits up takes a deep breath. "I will be fine, everyone. I just need some time to process this. Can you all just leave me here alone for a while? Uh, everyone except my mom and dad, I want them to please stay."

Tommy, Marnia, and Jonathan quietly exit the Land Cruiser and head into the building through the service door. With its loud echo throughout the garage, the door seems to slam shut. Jacob exits the vehicle and places his hand on the wall, like he's holding himself up, and continues to stare at it in silence. His mother and father also exit and stand on either side. After a few seconds, Jacob begins to weep bitterly.

Linda immediately grabs her son and holds him while Jim puts his hand on his back. Jacob turns to his mother, "I am sorry I never explained Cozumel to you. It's just when I saw what that animal had done to Marnia, and the dead girl on the kitchen work table, all the rage from the yacht incident came up as well. I truly never wanted to kill someone in my life until then. The commandant said I went through that animal like he was a cripple and he was right."

Jacob looks over at his dad. "He was good, Dad. I never fought anyone better, but the rage made me fiercer, stronger, and faster than I have ever been. Before I knew it, I was standing way up on that platform tossing him into the sea below. I knew what I was doing, and I recall making the decision to do it—even ordering Roberto and everyone else to stand down and leave me alone. But after it was done, I felt nothing. It was like a tease. He was just one of many, and now I find out he is the same one who has haunted me all these years. That yacht has defined me for half my life, Dad—how do I let it go?"

Jim's compassion for his son is palpable. He struggles to keep from breaking down himself. There's something he must say. Something he's kept in. It's hard for him to fathom revealing it now. He directs his gaze to his wife and looks deeply into her eyes. She knows the question. He doesn't need to say a word.

"Tell him," she says and then nods her head.

"Son," Jim says, "have you ever heard the old saying, the apple doesn't fall too far from the tree?"

Jim proceeds to tell Jacob the story of his investigation as a sheriff's deputy into a motorcycle gang's brutal rape and murder of several teenage girls in Story and Sheridan, Wyoming back in 1974. He was so close to being able to nail the gang with hard evidence that would have gotten most of them the death penalty back then. One night after he fought a group of them up behind the fish hatchery, eleven more showed up at their home on their Harleys. He told Linda to take Jacob, barely four at the time, and go hide out in the back of the house. He grabbed his Mossberg 500 12 Gauge shotgun and went out to confront the gang.

"Son," he says, "I walked out on our porch and saw those scumbags laughing at me. Two of them were suspects in one of the more brutal murders. I had a witness and the hard evidence that pinned them to it. We had warrants out for their arrest and were looking for them. At first, I tried to arrest them. Then they told me they were going to kill me and you and then do the same brutal thing to my wife that they did to the other girls. One of them pulled out a .45 and started shooting. Taken by surprise, I don't know how he missed me, but I dove to the side and when I landed I felt that same rage you described." Jim pauses and looks down at his feet a second. Jacob extends his neck waiting to hear the rest of the story. With glossy eyes, Jim looks back up.

"I killed five of those boys before I knew what happened. When I ran out of ammo I beat a bunch of them down with the butt end of the shotgun. Your old dog Thunder even joined the fight and took one out. But I would be dead if it weren't for your mother here. The leader of those boys pulled his bike around to the side of our porch and had his weapon out ready to shoot me. Your mother saw him and from the window twenty yards away, grabbed my Taurus .357 service revolver, pointed it out the window and fired twice. One of the shots hit the gas tank and it blew up right under that guy. Like you, after it happened, I felt nothing. It was just a tease. They were just some of the many animals that brutalize others."

"So, what happened?" Jacob asks.

"Your mother and I decided right there we had to leave. The sheriff wanted to promote me, said I could be sheriff someday. We said no. We took you and moved to Alabama and that's where I went to work for J. R. managing his detail and body shop. The rest you know."

Jacob stands up a bit more erect taking it all in. A grin breaks across his face. Then he outright laughs and says, "You fibbed to me, Mom. You told me all that noise was dad watching a John Wayne movie, and then you shot out the window and told me a wolf was trying to get into the house."

Jim reaches out and enfolds his wife and son in an embrace. He chuckles and says, "Well, the name of that biker gang was *The Wild Wolves*."

After the laughter subsides, Jim continues, "I guess what I am trying to say, son, is that you can't stop *all* the creeps in the world, but I do believe you can take care of the ones who try to hurt you and yours. You used a long chunk of your life to serve and protect other people. You did your best. You just have to trust that there are others who will do the same. Just make yourself realize and believe that there is always someone out there protecting people like you and I did, then it won't drive you crazy."

The truth in Jim's words penetrates Jacob's heart. A wave of relief washes over him. A huge weight, a burden, lifts from him. Years of heartache dissolve. He turns to his folks and says, "Let's go."

Manerez Private Jet Flying over Northern Mexico

Maximillian is frantic as he sits in his private jet rocketing to Falcon Lake. He knows the only leverage he now has that will keep Boris from killing him is Will Harrington. That stupid, self-important son of an even bigger idiot has no idea what he could potentially gain control over if he only really knew what he had in his hands. Few people were privy to Boris's organization and its inner workings. Max knew a lot more than Boris wanted anyone to know, including the fact that Boris took over all control of his family syndicate's money years ago. Without money, there is no syndicate, and he kept everyone on a shoe string budget by collecting all profits and dolling out only what he felt they needed. Over the years when people in his own family tried to take back control, they died. The only one left was Boris's brother.

Max's plan was simple—get Will and flee to Russia, then trade Will for asylum and protection. Will was next in line to control Boris's Western accounts in the Swiss banking system, then Boris's daughter Natasha and after that his brother. He knew Boris couldn't change the arrangement with the bank. The only way to eliminate Will from control was to…eliminate Will. If Max has Will, then he has the leverage that even Boris has to respect.

It's a race. He has to get Will before Boris and Natasha do. If he fails, it means his life. There's no safe place in the world he could hide. Unlike The Chameleon, Maximillian does not have an unlimited number of aliases and false identities to fall back on. Like Boris, Max is worth billions, but now that the United States government has proof that he imprisoned the Edwards for three years in Guatemala, and that he was the one who brought down the plane they were supposed to be on, he knew that a great deal of his assets would be seized and he would soon be without resources.

His private jet lands in a small unknown airfield out in the country, just south of his hacienda on Falcon Lake. A large Chevy Suburban waits for him with three of his most trusted people. Pedro jumps out of the Suburban and makes his way to the jet to greet Max and escort him to the vehicle. Max crawls into the front passenger seat, nods to the man and woman in the back seat, then says to Pedro, "We need to move quickly. Boris never got on his jet to Moscow and that means he is still in Mexico."

Pedro adds, "Boss, as you probably expected, all of our contacts in Boris's organization have gone dark. The buzz is that he and Natasha have called in all their people in Mexico and are headed this way."

Max wipes the cold sweat off his forehead with his handkerchief. After Santiago was taken down almost four years ago, Max absorbed what was left of his cartel not only for profit, but thinking it would give him more muscle to stand up to Boris. Now, cold reality is staring him in the face. His only lifeline is to get Will and get out of there as fast as possible. The reality that his son, Jonathan, chose Marnia over his own father is a betrayal he can never forgive. Like he did to Jonathan's mother before, Max is determined to reward his son's disloyalty in kind. All he has to do is get his hostage and make his way to Boris's brother in Moscow and everything would be okay. That's what he keeps telling himself, anyway, as he approaches his large hacienda on Falcon Lake.

He sees the hacienda's roof above the treetops, but the place is well secluded behind foliage, trees, and the perimeter wall. They pull through the gate and as soon as they clear the brush at least two dozen other vehicles and about a hundred armed men and women confront them. Pedro jams the Suburban in reverse only to find two large Hummers have closed the gap behind, blocking their retreat. Max sees Boris and Natasha emerge from the front seat of the vehicle and he catches a glimpse of Boris's nephew exiting the back seat with Will Harrington in tow. Peter throws Will to the ground in front of the Hummer and just behind Max's Suburban.

Though Boris has over one hundred guns pointing at Max and his accomplices, he is only armed with his walking cane, and his nickel-plated Walther PPK. Boris looks at Will, and then at the Suburban and yells, "Maximillian, I suggest you get out of that vehicle as quickly as possible. My patience is not that strong these days."

Max and his three accomplices get out of the Suburban with their hands raised. He stares at one of the few men in this world that he has ever truly been afraid of and wonders if he'll see another day. Boris smiles and points at Will. Max waits in silence.

"After much intense questioning" Boris says, "and with the help of my nephew, Peter, I have determined that this one has never betrayed me. Though he and his father were always overly ambitious, they were always too stupid to be of any threat to my plans."

Boris motions to Peter with his chin, who quickly helps Will to his feet to escort him into the complex to a holding cell in the basement. As they disappear into the door, Boris turns back to Max. "You, on the other hand..." he points his pistol at Max and puts two rounds into his left knee cap shattering it completely.

Max screams in agony and falls to the ground. Boris takes his walking stick and slowly withdraws the razor sharp saber hidden inside and places it at Max's throat. "You have been my best resource in this region of the world until now. I always knew you were smart, Max, maybe as smart as me, but like so many crime lords I associate with, you lack scope. You were a fool to keep Jacob Edwards alive. He is too well known and too loved by powerful people to ever think you could control him to use against me."

Peter comes back out of the hacienda and steps up beside his uncle. "Please, Uncle Boris, let me kill him. If not for him, our whole Western syndicate would still be operational."

Before Boris can answer Natasha steps up. "Peter, I love your enthusiasm, but we need to find a suitable replacement for Max before we kill him." She puts her right index finger to her chin, considers something for a moment, then seductively smiles at Max. "I believe Father wants to use Max here to lure his son, along with Jacob and his family, to his hacienda. Is that right Father?"

Boris once again feels the closest thing he can remember to a father's pride in a child. "Yes, Natasha, that is exactly what I want. Perhaps Jonathan would like his father's place. If not, we'll kill him too. But an attempted attack on that party will only end in failure. I know of this Captain Tommy Williams quite well. In my former trade, he was my equal, in killing and strategy. The only difference between he and I was his lack of ambition. When I retired, I went on to build one of the largest criminal empires of its kind in the world. He devoted himself to passing on his skills to law enforcement and military organizations. Jacob Edwards was his finest pupil, and as such, his pride and joy. That is why Maximillian here was so incredibly stupid to keep him alive. Once Tommy found out Jacob was still alive, there was no force on earth capable of stopping him, except perhaps me. But I was not aware of the problem until it was too late."

Natasha is visibly inspired by her father's insight and revelations. "So how do we proceed, Father?"

Holding the blade to Max's throat, Boris puts his other hand to his chin to think for a minute. "When hunting a grizzly bear in Alaska, I am told the hunter must lure the creature to hunt and then attack back in order to get a clean shot at a safe distance. If, on the other hand, the hunter tries to track and kill it, the bear will often double back and surprise and kill its pursuer. In my world, Tommy Williams is this grizzly bear. We have to get him to pursue us and coax him into attacking, and then we will be able to kill him with the rest of them."

Falcon Lake Highway Patrol Amphibious Unit
Docking Station

Carmen Garcia waits with her newborn baby, Natalie, on the dock at Government Cove, for her husband Willito to get off duty. Ever since the discovery of money smuggling going through Brownsville last month, the Highway Patrol special units on Falcon Lake are on high alert, and Willito, a boat commander, has been pulling a lot of double shifts lately. Carmen is still not over the scare of the failed assassination attempts on her, her husband, and his parents last month. If not for her quick thinking and God-fearing father-in-law Roberto, they would all be dead. These days, she does not feel comfortable without Willito, especially with a newborn first child.

Willito spies his wife holding their baby girl on the dock as he disembarks. The exhaustion of the last fourteen hours of grueling patrol work is forgotten. He tells his crew he will see them all at 8:00 a.m. sharp the next day and dismisses them. He eagerly dashes over to his wife and daughter giving them big hugs and kisses. Most of his crew want to go see their girls, so they are in their cars and gone almost immediately. Willito does not like to leave the dock until he is sure everything is in tip top shape, so he and Carmen walk around inspecting everything.

Carmen looks at her husband with sympathy. "I'm so sorry that the captain isn't giving you the time off to go see your sister, Mary, and meet your new nephew Roberto. Isabella called and said they are coming up tomorrow. When you get off work they'll all be here."

"That's great," Willito says, "let's get home right away so I can get some sleep and be ready for them. Maybe the captain will let me do a regular shift instead of all this overtime."

A very dark, sleek, and quiet yacht pulls up to the dock behind Willito's boat while he talks to his wife. Two figures dressed in black camouflage and carrying small Uzi machine pistols silently jump off the yacht and sneak up to the unsuspecting couple. Catching some movement, Willito senses danger and reaches for his sidearm. He sees lighting go off inside his brain when he is smashed in the back of the head with a heavy, blunt object. He blacks out. Carmen stands clinging to her one-month old baby with all her might, shocked by the suddenness of the attack.

Natasha flips her ski mask off and looks at Carmen with feigned compassion. "Mrs. Garcia, Peter here will help you aboard our yacht. Please just remain calm and compliant and we will take care of your husband. No further harm will come to any of you."

Garcia Home South Texas

Roberto sits in his prayer room thinking about his upcoming visit with Willito and Carmen, and his newest baby granddaughter, the following day. The thought of his family being whole again is something that is almost too good to be true, but Roberto serves a God of miracles and deliverance and what has transpired over the last few months has been a great witness of that reality. In the midst of his thought and prayer, a cold chill shoots up his spine and he feels and overwhelming need to pray for Willito, Carmen, and the baby.

Isabella rushes into the prayer room at that instant telling him that their children are in grave danger.

"I know," Roberto says, "let's pray."

They hold hands and focus on their children over on Falcon Lake. Thirty minutes later, Roberto is on the phone with Major John Brown and tells him about his deep concern for his son. John promises he will check it out immediately.

It only takes John a few phone calls and a few moments to find out that Willito and Carmen never made it home. John gets very concerned. Willito is of special interest to him, not only because he's Roberto's son, but also because Willito is in the process of joining the Texas Rangers. John knows talent when he sees it, and the youngest son of Roberto Garcia is definitely Ranger material. He is about ready to call Chuck Yeager when one of his Rangers pops his head into his office.

"Major, you better come out here and see what's on TV."

John heads out to the main office area where a large high definition flat screen TV hangs on the far wall. A local news station is reporting that Maximillian Manerez has just kidnapped Officer Willito Garcia of the Texas Highway Patrol along with his wife and child,, and is demanding safe asylum in the United States for their return. A picture of Willito, Carmen, and their baby daughter appears on screen. Carmen holds a Tokyo Newspaper with today's date on it sitting next to Willito in some type of holding cell, with the baby in her lap. Willito is incapacitated with bandages on his head.

John looks over at his IT guy and asks where the media got the picture. He tells him that it was uploaded to YouTube about an hour ago. John looks over at his Rangers. "Why are they using a Tokyo Newspaper to verify date and time?" All he gets are shrugs.

He pulls out his cell and taps Marnia's private number. "Marnia, John Brown here. Have you guys seen the news? Jacob's brother-in-law just got kidnapped, and it looks like Maximillian is requesting asylum in the United States for their safe return."

Rosemary Sargent's Hotel

Marnia and Jonathan are settling into their rooms when she gets the call from Major John Brown. She quickly tells him about her own predicament and Colonel Ramirez's betrayal. She heads to Tommy's room to get him involved. On the way, John tells her that he will figure out how to help them get out of Mexico City. Marnia raps on Tommy's door, pushes it open, and steps in. She is startled to hear the sound of a woman's laughter as she steps around the corner and sees Tommy and Rosemary quickly disengaging from what looks like some heavy nuzzling.

"Little girl," Rosemary says sitting up on the bed, "your timing was never something to brag about. What's up?"

Marnia tells the two what John just told her. Tommy hops off the bed and uses the remote to call up an American station on the TV. The same news report that John watched in South Texas is playing on this station as well. Tommy attentively studies the screen when the Tokyo newspaper flashes by. The color instantly drains from his face. He mutes the TV and tells Marnia to get Jacob and his parents right away.

Jonathan and Rosemary are disturbed by the look in Tommy's eyes, but neither says a word while they wait for the Edwards and Marnia to return, which happens in less than three minutes. The Edwards immediately recognize that Tommy is deeply disturbed. Marnia informs them about Maximillian kidnapping Willito and his family. Despite how crushing the news is, the Edwards are more concerned by Tommy's reaction and sense something far graver is at work here.

"Captain?" Jacob steps toward Tommy. "What's wrong?"

"Did I ever tell you about my father, Jacob?"

Jacob settles back a little and says, "Ambassador Rodney Williams. Yes, you told me the story. He was assassinated in an outdoor café close to the city park in Tokyo, 1976. You were there when he was hit by sniper fire. He died instantly. That's when you decided to join the new SEAL program the Navy was starting."

Tommy eyes everyone in the room and says, "Maximillian does not have your family, Boris does, and he also just told me that he killed my father."

Tommy points to the TV. Using the DVR feature he had already paused the frame on the Tokyo newspaper.

"Marnia, tell me, if you were investigating this, what would this newspaper clip say to you?"

Marnia leans into the screen. "Well usually when kidnappers use a newspaper in a photo with an abductee, it is to show the date that the picture was taken as a proof of life. But normally they would use the front page. This is page sixteen and it is a story about an historical café being renovated."

Jacob shuffles over to the TV and stares at the screen for a second. He points at the picture. "That's the café your father was killed at back in '76, right?"

Tommy nods.

Marnia adds, "So then, he tells the world that Maximillian has Jacob's brother-in-law and his family, makes everyone think he is using a foreign newspaper to throw them off his location, but in reality, he is baiting you with this new information."

"Marnia," Tommy says as he sits on the edge of the bed, "you are one top class sleuth." He gives her an enthusiastic thumbs-up. "Anytime you want to go to work in the states, you just give me a call, girl. Your insight is spot on. I only had a hunch that The Chameleon killed my dad. He was negotiating a trade deal back then with China that the old USSR was not happy about. We knew it was a KGB hit, just did not know enough to move on it. I joined the SEALs hoping I get a shot at the bastard who killed him. I honestly gave up on the thing twenty years ago when I gave up my team and starting training."

Jim joins the discussion. "So, you think this is some kind of trap?"

"Oh, I know it's a trap," Tommy says. "He wants me to head over to Max's place on Falcon Lake all half-cocked and get myself and all of you killed in the process. If it was just me, I'd already be on my way. But there's no way in hell I am sacrificing any of you over this."

Jonathan, who has been silently taking it all in, stands and gestures with his hand for everyone's attention. "I have lived in that hacienda where Boris now has Willito. I know every square inch of that place. It is similar to the Santiago complex where Marnia and I took him out. He may be trying to bait you, but I think we can do a little trapping of our own."

Intrigued by his postulation, Tommy looks up at him with some newfound hope. "Okay kid, I'll bite. What do you have in mind?"

Jonathan begins to lay out a series of unknown details about Maximillian's hacienda that few are privy to, not the least of which is a very elaborate cave system which tunnels under Falcon Lake into the United States and stretches south for about five miles.

Starr County Texas Ranger Headquarters

Major John Brown and Deputy Director Chuck Yeager are in John's office going over their plans to get Tommy, Marnia, Jonathan, and the Edwards out of Mexico City. Chuck sits in front of John's desk with a bewildered smile on his face. "So, are you saying that this brothel owner in Mexico City is harboring our people and she wants to have a parade through her part of town in honor of the Hero of Cozumel, so that we can use the distraction to get them away?" John agrees with Chuck how absurd the whole thing sounds but has concluded that it will be their best shot.

"Colonel Ramirez will only get away with arresting Marnia if he does it discreetly. The Cartel Crusher is just as popular, if not more so, than Jacob. If we work this right, the crowd will be so thick that that his troops won't even get near them and we can get them out and on the road before anyone is the wiser."

Chuck is starting to enjoy the idea of his friend finally getting that parade Mexico wanted to throw him thirteen years ago. "What about Tommy wanting to mount a rescue operation for Willito and his family? Do we really want Jacob, his mom, and dad involved in that one?"

John removes his hat and places it on the desk then starts to rub the tiredness out of his eyes. "I don't think we can stop them. I have tactical command on this side, but this whole operation is Tommy's baby, and that comes straight from the White House. Besides, that whole group down there is one hundred and fifty percent behind him."

Chuck leans forward. "What about those caves that go under Falcon Lake and come out in Starr County? Have you checked those out yet?"

John leans back and gives a big whistle as he exclaims, "Man that place is like Grand Central Station down there. We found forty seven illegals trapped down there waiting for someone to open the entrance on this side. With Max's hacienda on lock down, the whole operation was shut down and people were just left down there to die. I am pretty sure Max did not let Boris in on that little bit of intel."

Chuck leans forward and smiles. "You're telling me that Boris has no idea that there is a secret entrance to that hacienda from this side of the lake?"

John nods. "But, he has a small army over there. We can't ask for help from the Mexican military until this Colonel Ramirez stuff is taken care of. All the police on that side of the lake are in Max's pocket."

Chuck finishes the thought by saying, "which means they are all owned by Boris now."

John looks Chuck square in the eye. "We can't mount a military invasion into Mexico to rescue one highway patrolman and his family and Boris knows it. If anyone is going to make this work, it's Tommy. He, Jacob, and Marnia are figuring out a plan and are contacting me tonight on the details. In the meantime, you and I have to get their Mexico City extraction under way for this afternoon."

Garcia Home

Roberto, Isabella, Mary, Danielle, little Roberto, and Chris sit on the Garcia's front porch discussing everything that is going on. Roberto sternly addresses the group. "I understand that Chuck and John are doing their very best to get our family and friends home. I also know that Tommy Williams is the best in the world at what he does, but we can't put our trust in just them. God is the One Who is going to bring our loved ones home safe and sound. That is what we all need to focus on."

Danielle is holding little Roberto and stroking his hair as she says, "I know you're right, Grandpa, I just feel I need to do something more than pray. I want my daddy back with Grandma and Grandpa Edwards."

Chris grabs Danielle's hand.

Roberto says, "Captain Maelstrom and I got permission by way of Captain Phillips to help with the extraction. We join the team tomorrow morning in Starr County." He turns his attention to Danielle. "You are going to do more, Danielle, but you're going to do it with me. We will leave for Starr County with the others. Isabella, Mary, and little Roberto will stay here until we are done and will come when it's safe."

Isabella and Mary know when Roberto gives a final word and no objections were given.

Chapter Nine

Mexico City

Rosemary Sargent's Hotel, Mexico City, Next Morning

They threw together some floats and decorations pretty quickly. The designs are simple, but effective. Rosemary is ecstatic with all the commotion going on in the streets near her hotel. Considering the spontaneous nature of the parade, the turnout is huge. The float she will pull with her Cadillac convertible is made up to look like a cruise ship. On the sides are signs that say, "*El Cartel Trituradora*" and "*El Heroe de Cozumel*"—The Cartel Crusher, and the Hero of Cozumel.

She jumps out and runs up to Tommy. "What do you think of this?"

"Looks beautiful, baby," he says, "I can't wait for Jacob to get a load of all this. This is going to be good."

Jacob walks out clean shaven for the first time in three years and sporting a United States Commander's dress uniform. He takes one look at the float and turns back and starts to walk away. His mom and dad stop him.

"I know it's a little corny, son, but it's the plan to get us out of here. Just go with it."

Tommy is gleefully taking it all in, but especially enjoys Jacob's reaction and annoyance. "Kid, these people have been waiting a long time for this. Don't disappoint them." Tommy lifts his right hand and mechanically twists it back and forth like a beauty queen. "I believe this is the proper form for a parade wave, Jacob, better practice and get used to it before we start."

Marnia steps out with Jonathan and whistles at Jacob. "You cut that uniform very fine there, Commander. The years have been kind to you."

Jacob looks over at Marnia and smiles as he admires her in her military dress uniform with her Full Ship Captain insignia on her lapel and the Mexican Medal of Honor, *Condecoración al Valor Heroico*. "I couldn't be more proud of my own daughter, Marnia. You earned everything about that uniform. Don't you ever forget that."

Marnia is almost brought to tears as she kisses Jacob on the cheek and hugs him. "When I had Rosemary's people go to my apartment to get my uniform, I had them grab this as well." Marnia pulls out a little black velvet case from her purse and opens it up to show another '*Condecoración al Valor Heroico,* with Jacob's name on the insignia. "Since you never came down to receive this from our government my father gave it to me to keep. You know it can only be awarded by a ranking Mexican military representative or high government official. I received written permission from Presidente Rivera three years ago to present this to you."

Marnia steps back one pace and comes to attention and says in a strong and determined voice, "Commander Edwards, on behalf of the Mexican government and its people, for service and bravery above and beyond the call of duty, I, Captain Marnia Gonzalez, do hereby award you with Mexico's highest military honor." She pins the medal on his lapel, steps back again and salutes Commander Jacob Edwards. Jacob returns the salute as he thinks to himself that she is the only person in the world he would ever agree to receive that medal from. Everyone gives a big round of applause, then Jacob and Marnia take their seats on the float.

Tommy, Jonathan, and Jacob's parents crawl into the Cadillac pulling the float. Rosemary steps up to Tommy with a map of that part of Mexico City in her hand. They start going over the details of the route. Tommy places his finger at an intersection and says, "So you think this is where Colonel Ramirez will make his move to arrest Jacob and Marnia?"

Rosemary puts a sultry hand on Tommy's chest and rubs it softly as she says, "It is the most open part of the route. The highway lets in here and there's a large parking lot in front of the supermarket on the other side. That's why we're going to do the switch back here." She points to a spot on the map about two blocks before the open intersection.

Tommy grabs Rosemary's hand and kisses it, then pulls her head towards him and kisses her passionately on the lips. Rosemary pulls back. "The body shop finished the Land Cruiser last night. The paint is dry enough for travel. Now, you remember to come visit me the next time you're in Mexico City."

Tommy smiles from ear to ear and says, "I am already planning on it, babe."

Texas Ranger Major John Brown informed Tommy that he had some people in Mexico City who were going to help with the escape and who would show up around the same time as the switch. He briefed the others that when they were making their way to the Land Cruiser they would be backed up by John's people.

Rosemary gets into another Cadillac in front of them and activates its loud speaker system. Her driver pulls forward and she announces to the public that The Cartel Crusher and Hero of Cozumel are in the float behind them. Of course they would have never gotten official public notice for the parade, but even with their spontaneous announcement, it is one of the biggest she's seen. She is sure they caused quite a problem for the federal police and security forces in the city, which they intended to use to their advantage. Rosemary, with some help from a couple of associates very adept in social media, announced the parade on YouTube and all over Facebook and Twitter. It went viral. When they pull onto the main road they see the streets covered with eager onlookers, and even a couple of local TV stations.

The massive corruption of the police organizations in Mexico had been exposed a few years ago. Units like Marnia's Mexican Anti-Cartel Task Force were formed from the military to battle some of the larger cartels that were very adept at bribing and controlling police all over Mexico, Central, and South America. Today, that streak of corruption through law enforcement and security personnel worked in their favor. Many brothel owners in downtown Mexico City paid heavy bribes to local police for protection. The local units were out in force providing security for their clients which also became the kind of security their group needed as a buffer between them and the military forces under Colonel Ramirez trying to get to Marnia and Jacob. Two motorcycles and one car belonging to local police surrounded and followed the group with lights flashing.

Tommy sees Jacob and Marnia in the rearview mirror and both are waving to the crowd with smiles plastered on their faces. He almost runs onto the sidewalk at one point when the sight of Jacob doing a halfhearted parade wave leaves him in hysterics. The next block features a large crowd of children who appear to be on field trips from the local schools. The children start to cheer and throw flower petals at the two on the float. Children and teachers crowd the float requesting autographs on pictures they have of both Jacob and Marnia. One picture is of Marnia in front of the Santiago Hacienda after she pitched a battle with that cartel and came out victorious. Then there is the notorious picture of Jacob throwing the Jamaican off the cruise ship observation platform.

As the crowd starts to thicken, all the vehicles in the parade come to a complete stop and Tommy looks around back to Jim and Linda. "Get ready, this is the place."

A big Latino man appears out of the crowd and places a hand on Tommy's shoulder. He is with a Caucasian woman. "Captain Williams," the man says bending down, "I am Ranger Lewis Sanchez and this is my partner Ranger Rhonda Livingston. Major Brown sent us. Your vehicle is one block over and the decoys are on their way." Tommy turns around and sees a couple of remarkable body doubles that look just like Jacob and Marnia, being snuck through the crowd with ponchos over their clothing.

Jacob and Marnia make like they are interacting with the crowd of school children and exit the float. In the confusion of excited children wanting autographs, the body doubles quickly exchange the ponchos, wearing the same uniforms as Jacob and Marnia except for the Medals of Honor. The decoys get up on the float, four other replacements get into the Cadillac as Tommy's group exits. The parade continues as before.

The Texas Rangers escort the group into a laundromat where the ponchos are discarded and Jacob and Marnia quickly change into street clothes. Marnia hands her uniform to one of Rosemary's men who promises to keep it for her until she returns.

Jacob removes the Medal of Honor and shoves it in his pocket as he hands the man his uniform. The group exits out the back of the laundromat and Lewis points them to where the freshly repainted Land Cruiser is waiting for them. Rosemary's body shop changed the color from tan to sky blue, which is one of the more popular automobile colors in that part of the world. Jacob and his father are both excited about inspecting the job done to the vehicle as they hurry over. Jim looks at his son. "You think they remembered to get the door jams, engine, and trunk compartments?"

Halfway to the Land Cruiser eight street gang members pour into the street and surround the group. Lewis steps forward and confronts the closest one. "What do you want, hombre?"

The big one starts to laugh. "Colonel Ramirez said you would try to pull something like this, so he paid all the gangs in this part of town to watch you, and if you tried to escape, to keep you here until he could come and arrest The Cartel Crusher and the cabrón over there pretending to be the Hero of Cozumel."

Jacob and Tommy quickly take note that these street thugs have no firearms and have only brought knives and clubs. They look at each other, nod, and Jacob steps forward first.

The Texas Rangers begin to follow Jacob, but Tommy stops them and tells everyone to stand down. Jacob looks at the biggest one and sarcastically taunts him by saying, "I don't know where you're getting your intel from, buddy, but that's my dad and mom over there, and they will vouch for the fact that I am their bouncing baby boy, Jacob Edwards."

The big guy lets out a scream and lunges for Jacob with his large club. Jacob sees the move coming a mile away and lets the guy swing once at him, missing his face by mere inches. He steps into his assailant's perimeter, blocks the return swing with his left palm, and round kicks him in the rib cage with his right foot. He smashes him in the face with a wicked left hook, grabs the club out of his hand, thrusts the blunt end into his stomach, and then uses it to finish him with a blow to the back of his head. In the mere seconds that it took Jacob to finish off the obvious leader, three others gather their wits and attack. The first one is just stupid. He tries a full on frontal assault, lunging at Jacob with a knife in one hand. Jacob sees that his hands are held wide, so he throws a powerful front kick to the man's face knocking him out instantly.

The next two are a little more cautious as they approach Jacob from either side. The one on Jacob's right tries to take out

Jacob's kneecap with a wild swing of his big club. Jacob lifts his leg off the ground, and while it is in the air, whips a hood kick into the side of his face, followed by an immediate round kick to the other side. He grabs the man and throws him into his buddy who is lunging at Jacob to stab him with a knife. While the man is falling to the ground, Jacob manages to put him in a wrist lock and disarm him. He knocks him out with a sidekick to the face.

Jacob spins toward the remaining four assailants, giving them a silent challenge as he crosses his arms over his chest with the knife still in his hand. With barely a glance at each other, they scamper off in four different directions.

Tommy's group, relieved, heads for the Land Cruiser. "Hold up," Tommy shouts. He leans over the thug that Jacob threw into the other and sees he is still conscious. He looks at Jacob and says, "This one can't see us drive away."

Tommy kneels down, grabs his shirt, and knocks him out with a blow to the side of his face between the jaw and ear. He snickers at Jacob and says, "Geez kid, you could have left some for the rest of us. Instead you do the whole macho cross this line thing, and scare the crap out of them. Oh well, let's get the hell out of here before another gang shows up with guns."

By letting Jacob handle that gang himself, Tommy knew a message would be sent to all the gangs that Ramirez lied to them and that the Hero of Cozumel was really the one Marnia was helping. Tommy tells the group, "They'll tell their buddies that they got to see the man who defeated the Jamaican in hand-to-hand combat do his stuff."

While they pile into the Land Cruiser, Linda asks her son if he is okay. "Oh, I'm okay, Mom." He laughs and then continues, "Don't worry. At the first sign of losing control, Tommy would have stepped in."

Linda puts her hand on her son's cheek and laughs a little, then looks at her husband and says, "I guess all those boxing lessons you gave him and letting him do kickboxing in high school was a good idea after all."

Both Jacob and Jim laugh and Jim says, "Don't forget about letting him stay up late to watch the John Wayne movies with me."

"Yes mom, that was very important."

Linda gives a big old huff and crawls into the Land Cruiser. "You two are maddening."

The Texas Rangers get into a Jeep Cherokee with Texas plates and lead Tommy and his crew out of Mexico City. When they get to the outskirts of town, Jacob looks back at Marnia sitting next to Jonathan once again holding hands. "So, Marnia, why would those street thugs respect me but not The Cartel Crusher?"

Jonathan throws his two cents in. "Jacob, I've already told you what an animal Dominik was. He was a legend down here. Everyone thought he was unbeatable. But you easily beat him senseless, dragged him up to the top of the ship and hurled him into the sea. If this were ancient Greece, you'd be in one of Homers' classic tales. Marnia, on the other hand, wrecked one of their sources of income. Most of those gangs were on Santiago's payroll and Marnia here took him out. She's not very popular with them."

Jacob just shakes his head. "Well in my book, what you and Marnia did overshadows any stunt I ever pulled. Outside of saving her life, Cozumel was an act of a personal and selfish vendetta. From here on out I plan on never letting that vendetta define me again."

Both Jim and Tommy find great solace in what Jacob just said.

Tommy nailed it with the whole gang versus Hero of Cozumel thing. Within thirty minutes of the incident all the gangs Ramirez paid off stood down and went home. For the next few hours the group rides north in a peaceful silence.

Chapter Ten

La Hacienda

Maximillian's Hacienda, Falcon Lake

Boris stands on the dock of Max's hacienda, irritated as he waits for his yacht to arrive. He knows things are coming to a head and he needs what is on that boat. The silhouette of the boat manifests itself just outside the blanket of yellow light across the water of the lake, projected by the many spotlights around the dock. Boris allows himself to smile anticipating his precious cargo. The two most reliable ways that Boris motivates people is by the fear of death and lust for money.

As his men unload the crates from his docked yacht, he opens one up and stares at a whole lot of that second motivator. There are about a hundred men at his disposal in and around the hacienda, which under normal circumstances would be enough to handle any light covert rescue operation the United States may care to mount. But even with the help of Colonel Ramirez in the Mexican military, he knew that the kind of loyalty Marnia commanded could see him greatly outnumbered at any moment. He had to make contingency plans in case his confrontation with Tommy, Jacob, and Marnia went awry.

Natasha and Peter approach. "Father," she says, "Do you want us to take all of this cash now?"

"Yes," Boris says, "offer at least one thousand dollars per person willing to join us, and five thousand per child they can bring with them. Then, go to the local gangs and procure as much help as you can from them. You have two million in cash here. I don't care if you spend it all. Just get as much help as you possibly can."

Peter looks at the money curiously and then at his uncle. "Uncle Boris, are you positive this will work? Parents willfully putting their children in harm's way for money seems extraordinary to me."

Boris appreciates Peter's concern and replies, "About six weeks ago we paid a young boy one thousand dollars to have his leg mauled by a vicious dog in order to allow our assassins to gain entrance to the Starr City Hospital Emergency Room and he was overjoyed to do it. These people have never seen money like this before. Many are desperate. There will be plenty of volunteers."

Abandoned Lakefront Storage Facility, Starr County

Major John Brown is standing in front of the recently discovered entrance to a series of caves that run under the narrow outlet of Falcon Lake and into Mexico. Chuck Yeager, Captain Alex Maelstrom, Lieutenant Chris Rottanelli and Willito's two brothers, Thomas and Seth Garcia, are with him.

"You all know that what we are about to do is highly illegal" John Brown says to them, "The Mexican government has not granted any permission for us to go in and rescue Willito and his family. We know that Tommy, Jacob, Marnia, Jonathan, Mr. and Mrs. Edwards, and two of my best Rangers are on their way to the opposite entrance of these same caves in Mexico. The Mexican military is in turmoil right now with Colonel Ramirez trying to spread all that junk about Marnia. Boris certainly has some hold on him but we don't think it will last much longer.

Marnia is too well known and loved by her people to be in any real trouble. I wouldn't be surprised if some rogue elements of the Mexican military come to her aid at the hacienda if we need it. Our job is get to the hacienda, find Willito and his family, meet up with Tommy and his crew, and get back here as soon as possible. Boris and Maximillian are secondary. If we can snag them in the process and bring them over, great, but our priority is Willito, Carmen, their baby, and Tommy's crew."

Everyone nods their understanding.

Major Brown continues. "This whole thing started out as a rescue operation in Guatemala to extract Jacob, his mom, wife, and son from the Manerez Cartel prison. We have accomplished exactly half of that mission and we're here to finish the rest. I am told it takes about forty-five minutes to get to Max's hacienda going through these caves. We won't have radio contact with anyone during that time. Let's stick together and get this thing done."

Captain Larry Philips and Barbara are also present and will remain on the United States side of the caves as backup with a contingent of thirty military and law enforcement personnel.

John asks Larry, "Any news from the White House?"

Larry shakes his head. "The last communication I read from Vice President Rogers was that the state department is still in gridlock with Mexico. Whatever Boris has on Colonel Ramirez and others in the Mexican government is big enough to make them all clam up. Intelligence reports indicate that Boris was moved to the secret military facility from the state prison not to protect him from assassination by other prisoners, but to better facilitate his escape."

John chuckles and shakes his head. "You're not telling me anything I don't already know. Trying to get some of those peacocks to cooperate in honest law enforcement is like trying to saddle a mountain lion and go for a ride. Not happening. You guys just be ready, because a whole bunch of us could be stampeding back up that cave right there as we're chased by one mean Russian rattlesnake and his buddies."

Larry nods his head and assures John they will be there when he needs them. They shake hands and John returns to his group.

They enter the hole and begin their trek through the fascinating cave system under Falcon Lake. John is glad that he has Willito's brothers along on the rescue mission. They are both excellent lawmen and probably would make fine Texas Rangers, but they both seem content to work at the sheriff's department. John never pushes for recruits. They have to approach him with a lot of enthusiasm before he'll even consider recommending them. Willito, on the other hand, is different—a pure bullfighter that one. Two tours of duty in Afghanistan in the Marine Corps, one Bronze Star and one Purple Heart, the highest arrest record on Falcon Lake with the special boat patrol unit, he could track like a coyote and fight like a bobcat. John is eager to rescue the boy and show him what he has in his pocket for him when they get there.

South of Maximillian's Hacienda on Falcon Lake

Tommy drives on a dirt road five miles south of Maximillian's hacienda. They come upon and old ranch house that is built right up against a hill and stop. In front of the house are several Mexican military vehicles and about two dozen soldiers with an equal number of civilians kneeling on the ground with their hands clasped together on top of their heads, being held at gunpoint.

Tommy looks over at Marnia in the back seat with Jonathan and asks, "Are those your people?"

Marnia and Jonathan say "yes", immediately exit the Land Cruiser, and run up to the officer in charge. Jonathan vigorously shakes his hand and Marnia gives him a big hug. He returns it enthusiastically. All the soldiers face Marnia, come to attention, and salute her. Tommy and Jacob both take note of the tear in Marnia's eye as she returns the salute. As Jacob and Tommy walk toward the group, Marnia motions her officer to look over in their direction. "Captain Williams, Commander Edwards, I would like to introduce to you my second-in-command at the anti-cartel task force, First Captain Amilio Rohos."

Captain Rohos immediately comes to attention and salutes both men in front of him. "Commander Edwards, it is an honor to finally meet you, sir. All of Mexico is grateful to you for preserving the life of one of our most beloved daughters." He shakes Jacob's hand and then turns to Tommy and again salutes. "Captain Tommy Williams, my men are at your command. What are your orders, sir?"

Tommy returns the salute. "Captain, let's get these prisoners secured and then let's have a look at the cave entrance and the maps." Tommy is fluent in Spanish and easily begins to take over direction of the military personnel.

Marnia explains to the group that the location is built on the entrance to caves used by the Maximillian Cartel to smuggle people and resources in and out of the United States. She then sternly looks over at Jonathan and says, "A fact I have only recently been made aware of."

Jonathan just shrugs his shoulders. "My father never even told Boris about them. This is probably the best kept secret in all of Mexico, at least as far as cartels are concerned. Father never wanted to be solely dependent on Boris for his money smuggling operation. If Boris ever found out about these caves, he would have seized control, most definitely. I am positive that they remain unknown to him, at this time."

Rangers Sanchez and Livingston pull up to the group in the Jeep Cherokee and roll down the window. "Well folks, this is where we part company. Major Brown is already in the caves and I am supposed to let you know to meet him once you get to the hacienda entrance. I will take Mr. and Mrs. Edwards, go to Texas, and meet up with the backup force on the other side of the caves. Livingston is going with you."

Jacob asks, "Are you sure you can get my mom and dad across the border with no problems?"

Sanchez laughs and gets a huge smile. "Jacob, from what I heard, the president himself called the Mexican president and told him if anyone tries to hinder you or your parents from getting back into the United States, they are going to answer to him in ways they don't want to."

Tommy overhears the conversation and yells across the yard, "I think that'll do it. You sure you don't want to go with them kid? We can handle this."

Jacob shakes his head. "That's a hell to the no, Captain. I've known Willito since he was nine years old. One way or another, Boris Rasmov's persecution of my family stops tonight."

Tommy winks. "Suits me just fine, kid, I'd brave Heartbreak Ridge with you and you know it."

Jim and Linda step up to their son and give him hugs. With a tear in his eye, Jim says, "Just say the word, son, and I am with you. I may be old, but you know I can hold my own."

Linda pipes in. "If you go, I am going with you. You know that by now."

Jacob stares at his parents for a moment. "Dad, that evil bastard stole three years of our lives away from us. You and mom belong together. I am sorry, but I wouldn't be able to think straight if I brought you into this. You two go with Ranger Sanchez here and get back with the rest of the family. Pray for us. I will see you soon." Jim and Linda climb into the Jeep Cherokee and head for the border.

As the Jeep disappears down the road, Tommy starts to organize the next stage of the mission. First, he has Captain Rohos secure Maximillian's men in the barn adjacent to the farm house, then he has Jonathan show him the entrance to the cave. After ten minutes of studying the map and conferring with Jonathan, he figures they have about forty-five minutes to get to the hacienda and meet up with John Brown and his crew. Jonathan shows him on a hand drawn map the holding cells where Willito and his family are being held based on the picture in the newscast. Tommy, Jacob, Jonathan, Marnia, Ranger Livingston, and ten Mexican soldiers enter the caves and start to make their way to Maximillian's hacienda.

On the Road to Starr County

Roberto knows it makes no sense to bring Danielle along with him, but somehow, he also knows it is the right thing to do. He is walking with his trust in God, and his belief that if he and Danielle are not in the right place at the right time, disaster will ensue for all of them. Despite all that is at stake, Roberto feels a supernatural peace as he proceeds on the heavenly guidance he knows he is receiving. As they approach the dock on Falcon Lake where they are meeting the transport, he looks over at Danielle. "I know you are anxious, and might not understand what is going on, Danielle, but remember, as we keep God first in our thinking and priority, He will keep us peaceful so we can focus."

Danielle looks deeply into her grandfather's eyes with a trust born from experience. "You have taught me so much, Grandpa, and I know that what I learned from you about our lovingly heavenly Father is what saved me and Grandpa Jim on that yacht last month. I just want my family back, and I trust you. Whatever you want to do, I am with you all the way."

Roberto grabs Danielle's hand and tenderly kisses it. They both get out of his car and walk over to the dock where they are greeted by a familiar and friendly face.

John Bliss recognizes Roberto Garcia's Ford Fusion immediately and heads toward it as they park. John served as the communication officer on the *First Responder* commanded by Commander Jacob Edwards when it saved the cruise ship at Cozumel. When Roberto and Danielle get out, he can't help but smile at the thought of the Commander being alive and that he gets to help him and his daughter. "Chief, Danielle, it is so good to see you both. I got the local Coast Guard patrol boat to give us a ride to the other side. The commander was one of the security specialists under Captain Maelstrom on the *First Responder* when we served with Commander Edwards. He still doesn't know how you're going to get the Mexicans to let you disembark, but we have our ride and that's all you wanted, right?"

Roberto walks up to John Bliss and shakes his hand. "That is all I need, John, Thank you for your help."

John just grins from ear to ear as Danielle comes up, kisses him on the cheek, and gives him a big old hug. "Oh, I plan on going with you if you don't mind. I have not seen the commander in years, and if you two are going into danger, I want to help."

Roberto is very happy that John wants to help him. After the incident on the luxury yacht that John captained, he was hospitalized for a few days with a concussion. Roberto visited him every day and took the opportunity to teach him about God's healing power. John was released several days earlier than the doctors originally thought he would be. He then spent a couple of days at the Garcia's home where he attended his first Bible fellowship. It had such a powerful impact on him that he started attending a similar Bible study group in the Houston area where he lived. Roberto felt that with the three of them standing together in likeminded unity, they would get to see great deliverance wrought by God. Together they walk over to the Coast Guard Falcon Lake patrol boat and greet Chief Thomas Sullivan.

On the boat ride over to the Mexican side of Falcon Lake, Danielle cannot help but recognize the serendipity of the situation. She begins to make out the silhouette of the trees on the other side of the lake as they softly wave in evening breeze. Chief Sullivan tells everyone they will dock in five minutes. They pull into a completely deserted dock. Maximillian's Hacienda is just three miles east of that location with its own private dock on Falcon Lake, but for obvious reasons they avoid docking there. The Coast Guard lake cutter comes to rest. A few of Chief Sullivan's men jump onto the dock to secure the boat for the passengers to unload. Roberto thanks the chief for the ride and tells him he will call if he needs a ride back over. Roberto, Danielle, and John then disembark the cutter and walk through the completely empty facility to the road that leads to the hacienda. Danielle looks at Roberto and asks, "So what now, Grandpa?"

"Now we walk. It will take us a little under an hour to get there. We all need to stay calm and quietly pray in the spirit for God's protection and guidance."

As they begin the trek down the deserted road, they find a young teenage boy on a bicycle with a shoe shine kit on the back, riding toward the hacienda. Roberto asks him what he is doing and the boy tells him that earlier that day two foreigners with funny accents paid everyone in town thousands of dollars to go to the hacienda tonight and stay there for as long as they are needed. The boy missed getting any money, and was on his way to collect his share. Roberto reaches in his pocket and pulls out an American twenty-dollar bill, gives it to him and tells him to go home. He says there could be a huge gang war at the hacienda and it was not safe. The boy smiles from ear to ear as he shoves the twenty in his pocket, turns around, and heads back the way he came.

"Now we know why the dock was deserted." Roberto says to Danielle and John. "For some reason, Boris wants a huge crowd at the hacienda tonight." The three of them continue their trek. There is no fear or hate in the group for the enemy they are preparing themselves to face, just a dogged determination to do what is right.

Halfway into their trek, an explosion percusses the air. It comes from the direction of the hacienda, so the three quicken their pace, but Roberto will not let anyone run. Fifteen minutes later, they crest a hill where the three of them are stunned by the sight before them. Hundreds of men, women, and children are standing around the outside perimeter of Maximillian's hacienda with guards holding them at gunpoint. On the road ahead, multiple military vehicles are lined up and a least fifty soldiers are on the road facing the hostages, unable to penetrate the crowd of human shields before them. Roberto looks at his granddaughter and John Bliss. "No one panic. The first thing we have to do is find the officer in charge of the Mexican military brigade down there and introduce ourselves."

The Caves under Falcon Lake

Major John Brown and his company come to a stairwell that goes up the face of the wall about two stories high. At the top is a double steel door with a large platform before it. As the company begins to climb the stairs a very loud whistle comes from farther south in the tunnels. John uses his infrared binoculars to peer in the direction of the noise. As he focuses they come into view. He observes a party of about fifteen people and immediately recognizes the first man as Captain Tommy Williams. Walking next to him could only be Jacob Edwards, Marnia Gonzalez, and Jonathan Manerez. John is relieved to see Ranger Rhonda Livingston and about ten fully armed Mexican soldiers as well.

Before he can say a word, the two Garcia brothers have already run over and are hugging and slapping Jacob on the back. Jacob returns the hugs with equal enthusiasm. The three then walk back to the staircase arm-in-arm laughing and crying at the same time. John walks over to the trio and takes off his hat, extends his right hand, and says, "Commander Jacob Edwards, Major John Brown of the Texas Rangers. It is an honor, and might I say a great relief to finally meet you, sir."

Jacob enthusiastically returns the hand shake. "Believe me, Major, the honor is all mine. You're a big part of the reason I got my life back. I can't thank you enough."

Out of the corner of his eye, Jacob sees a very familiar and welcome face standing next to Alex and Chris. Chuck Yeager walks up with both arms extended and Jacob wraps him in one of his famous bear hugs. Chuck is laughing for joy so hard when Jacob grabs him that the hug almost knocks him out. Chuck catches his breath and looks up. "Well, I guess we finally figured out who that Russian James Bond was, huh buddy?"

"We sure did. Now let's go stop that evil bastard, okay."

John Brown heads over to greet Tommy Williams. "We're all here, Captain, and I see you brought some help. How do you want to proceed from here?"

Tommy looks over the whole group and is elated at the talent that is gathered under Boris's nose. "First things first, John, let's get up these stairs and open those doors. Jonathan here tells me that we might have to blow them open. I guess sometimes the illegals trying to get into the United States from here would get cold feet and try to turn back only to find that they could not. So, let's go take a look."

They assemble the group on the huge platform. Before them are two steel doors that are their only entrance into Maximillian's hacienda. Tommy tests the doors. "Yup, these babies are solid steel and locked with at least three dead bolts. We're going to have to blow them."

They hear some gunshots and people yelling. Jacob puts his ear to the door and listens. The group waits in hushed silence.

"I just heard Boris yelling at someone named Natasha to hurry up and follow him. He is going for help and they can take care of Willito later. He looks over at Tommy. "We have to get in there now."

Alex Maelstrom steps up with some C4 explosive and looks at Tommy for permission to proceed. Tommy nods his head and Alex applies the explosive to the spots where the deadbolts would be in the door along the seam between both doors. He attaches the remote detonator to it and tells everyone to step back and take cover. When the party is down the stairs and out of the blast radius, Alex hits the remote and both doors explode open.

"Lock and load people," Tommy yells, "we are going in."

Tommy and Jacob are first through the door, followed by Jonathan, Marnia, Chuck, Chris, John, Alex, and the two Garcia brothers. A huge rumbling shakes the room and before Ranger Livingston and the Mexican soldiers can step through some heavy steel barred gates fall in place of the doors that were just blasted.

Jonathan shrugs his shoulders. "I haven't been here in a couple of years. That's a new feature. My dad was always messing with new technology and gadgets."

Alex says to Tommy, "That's all the C4 I had. They'll have to go back to get more from Larry."

Tommy nods his approval and John tells Livingston to head up the tunnel until they run into Captain Larry Phillips and the others and get more explosives.

Rhonda then turns to the sergeant in charge of the soldiers. "Two of you stay here. The rest come with me."

The sergeant turns and looks at Marnia for confirmation and she says, "Go!"

Livingston leads the eight soldiers down the stairs and they start to make their way north to get the C4 to blow the bars.

Tommy motions the crew that made it through the blasted doors to follow him. The make their way to another set of doors. As they approach, they hear some kind of conflict taking place, which culminates in two gunshots. Jacob reaches up and clasps the handle to open the door, then looks to Tommy for permission. Tommy draws his gun and nods. When Jacob swings the door open the scene before them is almost too good to be true.

Maximillian's Hacienda Holding Cell

Two days after being attacked, Willito wakes up next to his wife and baby in a dimly lit holding cell. There is a sink and toilet out in the open on the wall behind them, and a single cot and a small stool to sit on. He sits up and reaches behind his head to feel the bandages. Carmen reaches over and starts to rub her husband's shoulders. "She hit you pretty hard, but the doctor they sent to check you does not think you have a concussion. She hit you below the skull on your neck. They kept you sedated until now. Why, I don't know."

Willito looks around the cell and sees another man across from them in a similar cell, middle fifties, medium build and strangely familiar. "Where are we?" he asks loud enough for the other man to hear.

The man looks up from the floor that he has been blankly staring at. "You are in the Maximillian Manerez Hacienda. Like both he and I, you are being held prisoner by Boris Rasmov and his daughter Natasha."

Willito is stunned by the news. His grogginess is starting to wear off and his focus is returning. "I know you! You're William Harrington, former Coast Guard Sector Corpus Christi commander. You were in charge of the Brownsville customs office until Boris's money smuggling operation was shut down. There is an FBI warrant out for your arrest. We have pictures of you all over our district."

Will looks up and tries to focus on the man talking to him in the cell across the hall. "And who might you be? I think I recognize the Texas Highway Patrol uniform, but I do not think that we have met yet."

Willito gets on his feet and vehemently stares at Will Harrington. "My name is Willito Garcia. You and your worm of a father betrayed my brother-in-law and tried to help Boris kill him in Cozumel, but failed. Then you helped Boris hire Maximillian to sabotage the plane that went down over the Pacific three years ago. We all thought my sister Mary, her husband Jacob, and his mother Linda were killed in that crash. But we now know that Maximillian stopped them from boarding that plane and kept them secretly in prison down in Guatemala until three days ago when they were rescued by a team led by Captain Tommy Williams."

Will is a little dizzy at the additional information he just received. In his long, painful interview he had with Boris earlier, the information about Jacob being alive and rescued was not shared. "You're Chief Roberto's youngest boy. I remember you. All three of you went into law enforcement."

Willito stands up and puts his face right in between the bars. "Yes, and I remember you, cabrón. You better hope I get a hold of you before my brother-in-law does. Not that I am going to be nice, but you know what he is capable of."

Carmen walks up to her husband and asks him to calm down. "He is in a cell just like us, Boris must not be very happy with him and yelling at him does not help us any."

The door to the room then opens and Natasha and Boris step in along with Peter. Boris looks over at the family in Max's holding cell. "It is a pity my hit team did not take care of you and your parents at the hospital. Now, things are going to be much more unpleasant for the three of you. It's good you're finally awake. I want to prove to the world that I have not killed you yet. Natasha, take their picture, Peter, hold the newspaper up against the cell so that the date is clearly seen in the picture."

Peter walks over and holds up a Paris newspaper in front of the holding cell where Willito and his family are, Natasha steps back to take the picture. After the third shot, Willito, with lighting speed, steps to the side where Peter is standing with the newspaper, sticks his hand through cell bars, and wraps it around Peters head and pulls back, ramming it into the bars. He reaches around with the other hand and grabs Peter's sidearm pulls it and points it at Boris and Natasha. "Now, cabrón, you are going to open this cell up and the both of you are going to take my wife and my daughter and me out of here. The first one to die old man is you, then the bitch standing next to you. Do what I say or I start shooting."

Boris can't believe his eyes. He wonders why the hell people are getting the drop on him so much lately. As he quickly goes over what just happened in his mind, he concludes that the three of them made no mistakes. The son of that Bible-thumper, Roberto, should not have been able to get to Peter so fast. He and Natasha should have been able to draw their guns. But Boris knows death when he sees it, and this Texas lawman is ready and willing to deal it out at any moment. "Natasha, hand him the keys to the cell, but stay back here."

Willito sees right through the plan. "Not so fast, Natasha. Mr. Harrington do you want to live? Because we both know that Boris here is going to kill you sooner or later. I can at least offer you a safe prison cell in an American maximum security prison."

Will is still stunned by the quick turn of events, but is coward enough to know that Willito is throwing him his only life line. "Yes, I do. What would you have me do?"

Willito smiles. "Okay, old man. I've heard about that stick you have in your hand there. Please let it drop on the ground and kick it over here in the direction of my wife."

At first Boris hesitates, but then sees that Willito is just itching for an excuse to kill him, so he complies. "Now, Natasha, I see you have a Glock 19 on your right hip there, please reach very slowly over with your left hand, and using only your index finger and thumb, pick it out of the holster, put it on the ground, and kick it over to my wife."

At first, Natasha looks like she is going to try something, but Boris looks at her sternly. "Natasha, this man wants to kill both of us very badly, the only thing holding him back is some sense of honor or duty. Do not test him."

Willito smiles. "For three years I thought my sister and her husband and his mother were dead. You murdered a plane load of innocent people, old man, and then you tried to kill the rest of Jacobs' family last month. Killing you right now would be the most satisfying of things, but my father did not raise me like that, but by all means, PLEASE give me an excuse to defend myself."

At that, Natasha takes her pistol exactly the way Willito instructed her and pushes it on the floor over to Carmen.

Willito looks back at Boris. "Now, old man, my niece Danielle told me how fond you are of that nickel plated Walther PPK, and I see the bulge under your coat." Willito raises the Glock 21 .45 caliber he took off Peter and fires. The shot enters the soft tissue of Boris's right shoulder just outside of the joint, taking a significant portion of muscle from that part of his arm. Natasha screams and starts toward her father, but is stopped by another shot coming from her own 9mm Glock that just misses her head and goes into the wall behind her.

Carmen is staring at her with the same vehement indignation her husband has. "That's also my family you have been trying to kill, bitch. Don't move."

Willito spent a lot of hours out on the pistol range teaching his wife how to shoot, and he is very glad he did. He looks back at Boris, "Well, I guess at the very least, your sniper days are over huh, old man? Now, with the only good arm you have, drop the PPK on the ground and kick it over here."

Boris had never been stupid or reckless in his life and he is not going to start now. He obeys Willito's instructions to the letter. Next, Willito has Natasha come over and open his cell door. He and Carmen step out and he makes her step inside and drag her unconscious cousin with her. He looks at Boris and motions with his eyes for him to join his daughter. As they are switching places, in more ways than one, a huge explosion rocks the hacienda.

Natasha sees the opportunity, pushes Carmen back and retrieves her pistol. Boris is right there with her and grabs his walking stick with his left hand. For a moment, the three are staring at one another, not sure of their next move, but Boris recognizes he is still at a disadvantage because Willito has Peter's .45 and his own PPK. Willito has already demonstrated that he is lethal with a firearm. Boris tells Willito that he does not want to start a gun fight in this room of concrete and bars because there is an infant in the room. As he is talking, he and Natasha are slowly easing toward the exit door to the room and she is pointing her gun directly at the baby in Carmen's arms.

Willito looks directly at Natasha. "You die first, then your father. Take that gun and point it someplace else, or we are going to have that gun fight your father is so worried about."

Boris can't believe what a wild animal Willito turned out to be. He is standing next to the door behind Natasha and he does the only sensible thing available to him. He grabs his daughter by the hair with his good hand and pulls her through the doorway, and then slams the door as they fall through. Willito fires a shot from both pistols as the door closes, but misses with each. Before anyone can stop him Peter is on his feet and follows Boris and Natasha out the door, almost knocking down Carmen in the process.

He hears the three scamper away and looks over to see his wife and baby are still okay. "We have to get out of here," he says to Carmen as he makes his way to the door to check the other side for any threats.

Will Harrington stands against the wall of his own cell flabbergasted by the turn of events that has just transpired in front of him. He looks over at Willito. "What are you going to do with me now?"

Willito looks at Will and sneers as he replies, "As much as I want to come in there and beat you to death, I need to take care of my family. You can stay there and rot for all I care." With that, Willito takes his wife and daughter and leads them out into the hall. There is a small stairwell that he surmises must go to the hacienda, and there is a set of double doors on the opposite side of the hall that has a Spanish "Exit" sign over it. As Willito is turning to go check out the exit-entrance doors, he hears a commotion coming from the opposite end at the top of the stairwell. He grabs his wife and child and quickly takes them to the place just under the balcony at the top of the stairs and waits.

Three men come through the door at the top of the stairs and run down. Willito can see that they are all armed. He quickly notices that Carmen is standing next to a light switch and tells her to turn it off on his signal. Willito learned in Afghanistan how to fight in cover of night, and he gained an uncanny night vision.

The three armed men get to the bottom of the stairs and Willito motions Carmen to turn off the lights. The room is instantly darkened. Without the light coming from under the three sets of doors, the room would be pitch black. Boris's three men are immediately disoriented, but not Willito. He quickly steps up to the closest man, grabs the wrist of the hand that is holding the gun, and twists it around and to the side. The aikido joint lock works perfectly, and the man drops his weapon. Willito smashes the man across the jaw with Peter's .45 knocking him out immediately. The other two are instantly alerted to the commotion and raise their weapons toward noises they hear. Willito had the good sense to attack them in a direction away from his wife and child, but sees he now has no choice, he must take them out quickly. He aims and kills the other two with the .45.

At that very moment, the double doors to the "Exit" open and Willito is greeted by the most fantastic sight he could ever have possibly hoped for. There in the opening of the door is a large group of people. Two of them he grew up with, one he has known most of his life, and one is someone he has been praying will be his new boss someday. Carmen sees the same thing and immediately turns on the light.

Thomas and Seth Garcia run up to their brother and his wife with Jacob close behind. The four adults and one infant have a quick, but emotional family reunion. Carmen walks over and hands her daughter to Jacob. "Jacob, I want to introduce you to your newest niece, Julia Isabella Garcia."

Jacob gently receives the beautiful little addition to his ever growing family. "Well, Carmen, this is one very beautiful little girl and she is very fortunate to favor her mother."

Willito walks over and pats his brother-in-law on the shoulder. "On that point, bro, you and I are in total agreement."

As usual, Tommy feels like the bad guy in the situation when he is forced to break up the family reunion and get people focused on the situation at hand. "I believe that we have what we came for. Everybody, back into the other room and let's figure out how to get that gate open so we can get these people home."

Jacob looks over at Tommy and then at Willito and begins to make introductions, but Willito pushes forward and comes up to Tommy. "Captain Tommy Williams, it is an honor to finally meet you, sir. I was a sergeant in the Marines in Afghanistan from 2008 to 2013. I have to say, sir, it's an honor to meet the living legend in the flesh."

Tommy sees the dispatched guards on the floor and says, "Well, seeing the three on the floor and the fact that you aren't in a holding cell, I'd say you didn't even need a living legend. Looks like you had things under control, Sergeant."

John Brown walks forward and puts his hand on Willito's shoulder. "We grow 'em good and strong here in Texas, Captain." With almost a fatherly pride he looks at Willito and continues, "Good to see you, the missus, and the baby are okay, Willito? I was pretty worried there for a while."

Willito stands a little firmer as he greets John Brown. They all head back to the exit area where the steel bars dropped in place after the doors were blasted. Tommy is there already and asks Alex to come and examine them. Alex steps forward and gets down on his knees so that he can see up the crevice from where the bars dropped. He uses the tactical flashlight from his utility belt to peer up into the crevice. "Looks like some type of hydraulic system is holding them in place, Captain. If enough of us pull up on them we might be able to raise them a foot or two."

Tommy, Jacob, Willito, his two brothers, Chris, and the two Mexican Soldiers on the other side all grab onto the bars and pull up with all their strength. To their delight, the bars begin to budge upwards, but the resistance is considerable. They manage to raise the bars up almost two feet. Willito motions Carmen to take the baby through first. He quickly follows them.

As soon as they are through a single gunshot comes from the entrance back into the other room. Boris, Natasha, and Peter stand in the doorway with several armed guards. All are pointing weapons at the group, except Boris. Only Willito, his wife and baby, and one soldier made it through the bars to the stairs descending into the caves below.

Boris's right arm is in a sling with his shirt sleeve cut off to make room for the bandages on his shoulder. He scans the room and then looks directly at Tommy. "Tell your people to lower all their weapons to the ground and push them in front on the floor. Then very carefully lower those bars back to the floor. I had a little conversation with Maximillian in the infirmary. He enlightened me to the presence of these caves. Just another secret he kept from me. The entrance to the caves here has a failsafe on it. If someone persists in trying to get through those bars after the doors are removed, an explosion will be triggered that wipes out this room and a part of the cave system below."

Tommy's pretty sure it is not a ruse and they let the bars back down to the floor. Boris smiles and then sneers. "Now where is that little maggot who shot me?"

Jacob steps forward and says, "You know Boris, I never did like you even when you were just another New York auto dealer. My brother-in-law who took a chunk out of you is on his way back to the other side of those caves. When he gets there, he is going to tell a whole lot of people what's going on here. That's why I am not afraid of you right now. The only thing standing between you and them is me and my friends here, so you need all of us very much alive."

Boris looks at the group standing with Jacob. "You are quite correct in assuming that I need, you, Tommy, Marnia, and maybe a few of the others for insurance, but what's to stop me from killing the rest?"

All the people in the group that Boris just mentioned step forward and use themselves as human shields for the rest.

Jacob then says, "You open fire now and we'll be the first to die, but somebody is going to get to you, or one of the two governments you just pissed off will get you. I believe we have what they call down here a Mexican standoff. Your call Boris."

Natasha, standing next to her father, feels her phone vibrate. She glances at the text. A look of horror comes over her face. "It's too late," she screams at her father. "The trigger tripped, Max's men say it's going to blow in less than thirty seconds." She turns and dashes up the stairs with Boris and Peter following, then their contingent. Tommy's group follows as well having nowhere else to go. In the mad scramble, Tommy and Jacob manage to swipe a firearm off the floor, as do a couple others. By the time the last of the party gets up the stairs and into the hall beyond, a massive explosion rocks the very foundations of the hacienda.

Tommy, Jacob, Marnia, and Jonathan are the first through the door after Boris's people who vacated in another direction and are nowhere to be seen. They find themselves in the main hallway of the hacienda. Jonathan points to a set of double wooden doors on the opposite end of the hall and says that is the way out. The group proceeds cautiously as only four of them are armed.

Chapter Eleven

A Greater Judge

Main Road Leading to Max's Hacienda

Roberto, Danielle, and John Bliss make their way up the road that runs past Max's hacienda. Roberto stops and asks one of the Mexican soldiers who is in charge. The man points to a Jeep in front and says, "Captain Rohos." As they head toward Rohos a soldier uses a shoulder mounted missile launcher to fire on the wall that surrounds the hacienda. The impact sends a shockwave through the earth at least a tenth of a mile in every direction. The men inside the perimeter are ready for this and begin to force some of the families from the court yard to the gate of the wall where they are easily seen.

One of Boris's men gets on a loud speaker and tells the Mexican military that they have over one thousand women and children inside and if they attack again, they will start killing them and throwing their bodies out into the road. A Mexican soldier halts Roberto and his companions while they await an order to attack or withdraw. No such orders are given. After twenty minutes Roberto is led up to Rohos's position.

Captain Rohos tells his men to stand down and wait for more orders. As he turns, he is met by Roberto. "Excuse me, Captain, my name is Roberto Garcia. My son and his family are the ones that were kidnapped two days ago by Boris Rasmov and are being held in that hacienda right now."

Amilio recognizes Roberto from pictures that Marnia showed him of Jacob's family and does not even bother to ask how he got on this side of the lake. He assumes that Marnia had something to do with it. "Yes, Chief, I know of you very well. This is Captain Marnia Gonzalez's battalion and we are here to back up the rescue teams in the caves."

"Captain," Roberto says, "it is of the utmost importance that my companions and I get into that courtyard as soon as possible." Amilio stands there in disbelief at what he just heard. It is, in Amilio's opinion, one of the most bizarre requests, under the circumstances, that he has ever heard. He scans the group and immediately recognizes Danielle Edwards, but has no clue who the other guy is.

"Chief, I can't let you put Jacob's daughter at risk like that. All those people are being held hostage by Boris's henchmen and they just threatened to start killing them if we show anymore aggression."

Roberto puts his hand on the young officer's shoulder before him. "Captain Rohos, I was there on that cruise ship the night Jacob saved your commanding officer's life. I helped to take care of her and her companions after he killed that Jamaican. This Boris has been trying to kill Jacob and his family since even before that time. If I am not in that courtyard soon, tonight he will succeed in finishing the job he started over thirteen years ago and Jacob, Marnia, and the rest will be dead."

Amilio is stunned by the words, the boldness, and the surety of Chief Roberto Garcia. Held by his intent but commanding gaze, he can see the truth of the words in Roberto's eyes. "I will do what I can to help you, but I don't see how it is possible. There is only one way in, and it is blocked by a human shield."

"My God will give me a way in." Roberto says, "I just ask that when it comes, you don't try to stop me."

Another even larger explosion shakes the entire area like an earthquake as soon as the words leave Roberto's mouth. Some parts of the wall crack and topple. The front gate erupts in complete confusion. Panicking hostages flee in every direction, many flee into the road toward where the Mexican military is positioned. Other personnel and prisoners make a mad dash away from the wall. People run all over the place. In the chaos, Roberto, Danielle, and John Bliss simply walk into the hacienda courtyard and mingle in.

Back Inside the Hacienda

As Tommy and the crew make it to the front door and prepare to exit the hacienda, several doors open on both sides of the hall and heavily armed thugs pour out holding them at gunpoint. As if on cue, out steps Boris, Natasha, and Peter to the front of the group. Boris stares intently at Tommy and says, "Now, where were we? Oh yes, you all were threatening me." With his left hand Boris quickly puts a round into Tommy's right shoulder with a small semiautomatic pistol.

The escaping party can do nothing with all the weapons pointed at them. Tommy drops his firearm and grabs his shoulder as he leans against the door he was trying to exit. Boris sneers at him. "When I killed your father, I thought about putting you out of your misery as well. Oh well, they say hindsight is always twenty-twenty."

As Boris takes aim again, like lightning, Jacob lunges forward and manages to twist behind Natasha and put her in an arm lock while cupping her chin with his other hand. "Don't even think about it, you bastard." Jacob says to Boris, "That's my teacher right there and if you pull that trigger, you'll get to see how fast he taught me to kill someone with my bare hands."

Marnia and Jonathan reach around and open the door. Still facing Boris and his men they slowly back out into the courtyard with Tommy. With full focus on the threat before them, they miss the threat behind until they hear a bolt lock and load and Marnia turns to see at least fifty more armed men aimed and ready to fire.

She stops.

"Jacob, let her go." She says, "It's hopeless, we are completely surrounded."

Jacob lets go and Boris's men quickly disarm the party and usher them outside. Boris steps out onto the entrance of the hacienda that looks out over the large courtyard. Someone brings a chair for him to sit on so that he can rest his shoulder. With a mocking compassion he says, "Please get the good captain over there a chair as well. We would not want him to become too fatigued just yet. I believe I do owe him a little professional respect. After all, he is one of the very few people in this world who is as effective an assassin as me."

Tommy scoffs. "I was never anything like you, you, sick bastard. I only killed to save lives and defend my country."

"Tell yourself what you want, Captain," Boris says, "killing is killing, and there is great power in dealing out death in the way we do. I have simply learned to not just live with it, but to serve it and reap its many rewards. But there are others who have not yet learned to serve it as I do, and I think it is about time to remedy that flaw. Natasha, Peter, come here."

Boris's daughter and nephew step forward. Boris looks at his daughter. "How long before Peter's father arrives to pick us up?"

Natasha checks her cell phone clock. "If he is on schedule, another hour, Father."

Boris sneers at Jacob with an evil gleam in his eye. "That should be plenty of time." He turns his attention back to Natasha and Peter. "You two are the only ones in the whole world who could possibly run my empire someday. But even you have failed me tonight. Peter, you should have never let that little maggot Willito disarm and incapacitate you so quickly. Natasha, your famed Hero of Cozumel caught you completely off guard earlier and made me look like a fool. Both of you are going to redeem yourselves in front of me and everyone here. Now, since Willito is not here I am going to choose a replacement. You are going to kill Commander Jacob Edwards, the so-called Hero of Cozumel, and Captain Marnia Gonzalez, The Cartel Crusher. And since Jacob here was going to use his bare hands on you, my dear, that is all you are going to get to use on them."

Jacob is flabbergasted at the barbarism of Boris's idea and steps forward. "Why do you think Marnia or I would even agree to such a thing?"

Boris looks over at the group and points to Chris and Jonathan. "Bring those two over here." He then looks back at Jacob. "Because if you do not, I will start by killing these two."

Chris blurts out, "Don't do it, Jacob! He is just going to kill all of us anyway."

"Not true, young man. There is a small speed boat docked in back here. If Jacob and Marnia win the contest, I will allow you two and Willito's two brothers to take it and go back across the lake."

"And if we lose, then what?" Jacob asks.

Boris sneers, "You will be dead, of course, and the rest will come with us as hostages."

Jacob looks over at Marnia who simply nods her head to say yes. He stares vehemently at Boris.

"Okay, let's do this."

Boris looks at his daughter and nephew. "Do not let me down again. Kill them and be done with it."

Boris then gets a devilish gleam in his eye, looks over at Jacob and says, "Dominik Thrace was one of my best lieutenants in South Mexico and Central America. He helped me keep the cartels compliant. You took him from me. I put Peter here in his crew when he was barely sixteen-years old. Peter was the third person on that pirate crew that attacked the yacht and butchered the Mexican finance minister and his family back in 1996. Dominik trained Peter for years in hand-to-hand combat. I myself have taught Peter how to kill in countless ways. I would say that Peter is an even more formidable opponent than Dominik was. He is now thirty-six, and you almost twenty years his senior. Good luck, Jacob."

With guns pointed at them and all their friends, Jacob and Marnia step forward to face Peter and Natasha. Jacob looks over at Marnia. "Danielle told me she has anger issues and can be taunted. Plus, she can't take power strikes to her midsection very well."

As the four face each other waiting for Boris to signal a start, they are silent and completely unreadable. Boris looks at the four in the courtyard and yells, "Begin."

Peter takes one fast look at Jacob, grabs Natasha, and throws her into him, then attacks Marnia with a devastating right cross that just barely misses her jaw as she tucks it into her chest. It lands on the thick bony part of her skull. Peter lets out a yell from the pain and Marnia comes up underneath his guard and slams the top of her head into Peter's jaw. Peter is thrown back by the power of the impact and loses his balance, falling on his back. Marnia is instantly on him, and starts to rain down blows as the two begin to engage in an MMA-style ground fight.

Natasha, shocked by Peter's tactics, manages to push herself away far enough to round kick Jacob in the head with her right foot. Although it is a powerful kick that momentarily stuns Jacob, Natasha is only wearing sneakers, unlike when she buried the steel toe of her high heeled boots into Captain Bliss's temple on the luxury yacht over a month ago. Jacob knows he needs to make quick work of Natasha before Marnia gets into too much trouble. He drops down to the ground as she tries to follow through with a turning sidekick and sweeps her support leg out from under her. He then summersaults over to her position, grabs her by the hair, and sends two piston-like punches into her upper jaw line below the ear knocking her out. He then kip-ups to a stand, turns and bolts over to Peter who is now sitting on Marnia with both hands crisscrossed over her throat using the collar of her shirt to squeeze and choke her to death.

Before Peter sees him coming, Jacob manages to square up and round kick him in the nose shattering it and knocking him off Marnia. But Peter uses the momentum of the blow to catapult himself over and up into a standing position. He is close enough to jump straight up and throw a devastatingly powerful crescent kick into the side of Jacob's face. The force of the blow is enough to take Jacob off his feet. He flies sideways onto the pavement but twists and lands on all fours where he tries to catch his breath.

Peter comes in fast behind but Jacob, totally aware, throws a right mule kick at Peter's groin. The impact of the kick knocks the breath out of Peter, but he still manages to catch the foot before it fully impacts his groin. He then goes for a counter kick between Jacob's legs while holding the attacking foot. Jacob does a quick whip-like turn with his body and Peter's kick flies wide. Balancing on his hands, Jacob uses the leverage of Peter's grasp on his leg to launch his other foot and throws a heel kick into Peter's broken nose. Peter screams from the pain and lets go of Jacob's leg as both his hands cover his bleeding nose. Jacob's leg slips out and he falls backward hitting his head on the cobblestone.

Natasha comes to, shakes the dizziness out of her head, then pushes herself up to her feet unnoticed by Jacob or Peter. She draws a switchblade from her back pocket and ejects the knife with a quiet click. She sneaks up on Jacob whose intense focus is on Peter as he sits up. Coming in from behind and crouched like a cat in silence and in stealth, Natasha closes the distance. Before attacking, she glances at her father who gives her an approving nod with a wicked smile.

Marnia can't remember if she'd ever been choked like that. Her throat hurts terribly but she is breathing normally again and lifts her head to assess the situation. Seeing Natasha about to leap upon Jacob with the blade fills Marnia with a sudden surge of urgency. She springs to her feet and lunges for Natasha who becomes aware of this new threat in time to sidestep Marnia and swing the blade at her. Marnia pulls back and feels the air from the tip of the blade swish by missing her cheek but it lightly slashes her forearm drawing blood. It's mostly a surface wound but Marnia is none too pleased as she ducks low and swings her body to the right with renewed focus while pulling her right knee deep into her chest. At the end of her turn she catapults an explosive kick into Natasha's midsection, doubling her over and sending the knife flying from her hand. Marnia steps in, grabs Natasha by the hair, and rams her face into her knee several times until Natasha drops unconscious again.

"Stay down this time," she says, sneering at her foe. She swings around to help Jacob but finds that Boris's men have intervened and flanked her with their weapons trained on her. Jacob turns toward Marnia and they lock onto each other's eyes in an extremely profound earnestness unlike any either has ever felt. Marnia chooses wisely to refrain from physically aiding but shouts, "He's the last scumbag from the minister's yacht, Jacob, finish him off and be free from it once and for all."

Jacob gives her an unspoken "thank you" and regains his feet as he returns his focus to Peter who is already on the attack. Peter slams into Jacob and pummels him with strong punches to the face. The first three or four land pretty solidly, but truth be told, this is Jacob's element. Of all his martial skill, Jacob is first and foremost a fist fighter. He instantly figures out the rhythm of the punches coming at him and blocks each one with simple slaps to the side. Then he attacks. Jacob's punches are short, straight, powerful, and rapid like the revving pistons of a gasoline engine. He throws blows to the face and the body. Peter doesn't have a chance now; he has simply become a punching bag. Jacob begins to feel bones break under his fists—first some ribs, then Peter's jaw and teeth.

Peter's arms sag leaving his face and body completely exposed to the fury of Jacob's assault. The last time he beat someone this badly was on a cruise ship at Cozumel. But Jacob is not in a rage now, not even with this third crewmember of that horrendous assault on that thirteen-year-old's family. No—the incident no longer defines him. He is in control of what he is doing and he is meting out a righteous punishment. The fact that this man almost choked Marnia to death burns on his mind, but he's not going to lose it this time. He pummels Peter only until Peter collapses and drops onto the pavement, an unconscious pile of broken bones and bruised meat.

A type of serendipity goes through him as he remembers dragging Dominik Thrace up that ladder to his death. He lets out a deep sigh and with a riveting gaze says to Boris, "I am done punishing and killing, Boris, there is no vengeance left in me. I will always defend those I love, and try to stand up for what I think is right." He points an accusing finger at Boris. "That yacht doesn't define me anymore. What you let that animal and your nephew do to that family is on you, there is a greater Judge than I and that blood is upon your head. The full payment for the death and hatred you deal will return to you. I am done."

Boris's face contorts in a rage as he pushes himself from his seated position in front of the hacienda and raises his gun to point it at Jacob. "Death is the only true power, Jacob. It is permanent and absolute. It has solved every problem I have ever had and made me into an emperor. And now, I am going to finish what I set out to do thirteen years ago." Boris aims at Jacobs's skull and softly says, "Goodbye, Commander Edwards."

"STOP IN THE NAME OF JESUS CHRIST." An all too familiar voice sounds out from the crowd. "YOU ARE FINISHED!"

Words too powerful to ignore. Words tolerating no disobedience or obstruction. Yet they are just simple words, uttered by a simple man. As if a thunderbolt of lightning explodes from the heavens above combined with the fresh cleansing scent of ozone in the spring air, something pops in Boris's head and he can't pull the trigger.

Roberto Garcia—a man, a husband, a father, a grandfather, and a minister of the gospel—steps forward from the crowd of hostages. He is accompanied by his granddaughter, Danielle, and his spiritual brother, John Bliss. All guns are lowered and everyone steps aside as Roberto leads his companions up to the entry level of the hacienda where he stops and looks into Boris's petrified eyes. With the power of the Almighty coursing through every fiber of his being, he raises his palm towards Boris and says, "You evil, worthless son of darkness—you who worships death and serves the father of it, the God of light now gives you over to your master and death will give you only what it can."

Boris's look of astonishment and confusion is profound. With his arm still extended, locked in place, the color drains from his face. He convulses slightly as his strength fades and the light dims. The gun drops from his hand and he simply falls back into his seat, closes his eyes, and never opens them again.

At first, there is a hushed silence over the entire crowd. Several of the hostages do the sign of the cross touching their forehead, sternum, then left and right shoulders followed by folding their hands in prayer. Even Captain Rohos and his men out on the road know something extraordinary has just occurred. In unison, Boris's and Max's men begin to throw down their weapons and raise their hands in the air. Natasha and Peter lay unconscious on the cobblestone courtyard and Maximillian is secure and sedated inside the hacienda. There is no one to take command. One of Max's men acknowledges Jonathan and looks to him for guidance. For the first time ever, Jonathan seizes complete control of the Manerez Cartel and steps forward.

"It's over," he announces with a commanding stare. "Leave your weapon's behind and go report to Captain Rohos and his men." He points out at the outer road where Rohos's forces wait. A few begin to respond and before long most are following with their hands on their heads. Jonathan nods in approval then heads over to Marnia to help her.

Jacob, completely speechless, stumbles over to Roberto and with tears in his eyes gives his father-in-law a hug. After a moment he pulls himself together and says, "It's always been you, Pops. You believed and trusted God when the rest of us just skidded back and forth. You were the one who kept Boris from killing me at Cozumel, and you just did it again."

Roberto smiles at Jacob and the rest and says, "No, Jacob, God is the One who saved you both times, I am just the son and servant fortunate enough to hear and obey His voice."

The entire group begins to draw in and gather around Jacob and Roberto as they try to understand what just happened. Some are perplexed. Danielle also. She looks at her grandfather and says, "What happened, Grandpa? Did God kill Boris?"

Roberto looks lovingly into his granddaughter's eyes but says loud enough for all to hear. "God is all love and all light and did not kill anyone here. Boris, by his own mouth, confessed that he served and worshipped death. He gave death credit for all the great things in his life. Even as Jacob uttered by inspiration, '… that blood is upon your head. The full payment for the death and hatred you deal will return to you.' God simply allowed death to have him. Boris was not just our enemy, he was God's enemy by his choice. Boris chose that dark path a long time ago and he gave himself to it. It is a road from which one cannot return. In the Old Testament, men like Boris were called sons of Belial, worthless ones who chose to shun and deny the true God and instead sold their souls to the serpent through his false gods."

Roberto turns and sees a small crowd still lingering and listening to him. He directs his voice at everyone in earshot. "If any of you would like to know more about these things, my door is always open, you are invited to come and see. But right now, it's been a long and trying day. Let's all go home."

As Roberto finishes speaking, several trucks full of Mexican and U.S. military forces pour into the compound.

"Well," Tommy says, "it looks like the president finally got Mexico to come to its senses, here comes the cavalry. We'll have to tell them that the real cavalry already *came*."

*　*　*

Out in the middle of Falcon Lake, a lone yacht, not unlike Boris's, lays anchored. A man who seems to be a younger version of Boris stands on the deck looking at the hacienda with high-powered night vision binoculars. Another man approaches him and says, "Reuben, do we dock and try to rescue your son and niece or do we leave?"

Reuben looks at his man. "We leave. Peter and Natasha chose their path. They followed my brother to oblivion. We are going back to Moscow and I never want to see this part of the world again. With Boris gone, we are all free to pursue our hearts. Mine belongs in Russia, not here." The anchor is pulled and the hi-tech stealth yacht quietly surges away and its passengers are never to be seen in the Western world again.

* * *

As the Mexican and United States military begin to arrest all of Max's and Boris's men in and around the hacienda, William Harrington is found still alive in his holding cell. When he disembarks the transport that takes him to Starr County on the other side, the authorities parade him by the Edwards and Garcia families. Jacob just stares at his former commanding officer with a disgusted look on his face, but his wife Mary breaks away from the crowd to encounter him, and she looks him straight in the eye and says, "You bastard." She then takes her right hand up to her left ear with the palm facing out and using her whole body she whips her backhand into his left cheek bone knocking him to the ground. She turns and on her way back to her husband and daughter says, "A little trick Jonathan taught me."

Later that Evening in the Starr County Hospital Emergency Room

After Max, Natasha, Peter, and others are arrested, Captain Marnia Gonzalez finds out that she is now the ranking officer in the Mexican Anti-Cartel Task Force. Colonel Ramirez was arrested earlier that day for having been on the payroll of Maximillian and Boris since the inception of the force. She uses her new authority to let Deputy Director Chuck Yeager and Major John Brown take Peter, Natasha, and Maximillian to the United States to be charged with a myriad of crimes. John Brown's Texas Rangers guard Maximillian as doctors inspect and work on his knee.

Jonathan stands in the room with his father, who is not very happy with his son's choices.

"What do you expect now, you silly idiot?" Max says, "Are you just going to live with that Mexican cop and be her house maid or something? Everything we have will be seized by governments and other cartels. You basically have nothing."

From the doorway to the room, a solemn voice interrupts their conversation. "He has a mother who loves him, and wants him back."

All eyes turn to the doorway where Major John Brown is standing next to a strikingly beautiful woman in her middle fifties. Those who know John also know the woman next to him is his longtime wife, Susan. Jonathan and Max both stare at the woman for a long somber moment and Jonathan finally says, "Mother?"

Max looks at Susan Brown and says, "This can't be! You died almost thirty years ago. My men told me you were dead and buried over here in Starr County."

"Yes," John Brown says, "I ran into those varmints that night and they would have killed her, but let's just say I kind of persuaded them otherwise. At first, I was going to use her as a witness to put you and your father away. But she was so concerned about Jonathan here that she convinced me to let the varmint go and let them lie to you about her being dead. They knew if you found out she was still alive you'd kill every one of them. Susan and I fell in love and I married her. Since then, I have been hunting you and looking for a way to legally take you down so that she could get another chance to be with her son."

Max lies motionless in his bed and stares at the woman who betrayed him and got away with it. His pride won't let him say another word.

Jonathan steps over to the bed and peers down into his father's eyes. "Goodbye, Maximillian Manerez. You will never see me again, except for maybe in court. You are no longer my father and you deserve anything they do to you. Only a coward would have the mother of his child killed out of spite."

He then looks at his mother. "There are so many things we need to talk about, but not here."

John nods his approval to Susan and to Jonathan and the three walk out together.

Before the trio leaves, Jonathan calls Marnia on the phone to tell her the extraordinary news. She is so astounded by all the fantastic things that have happened in the last twenty-four hours that it's hard for her to process it all. With tears of happiness, she tells him how overjoyed she is for him and that she will talk to him in a day or two after she sorts out official State business.

Major John Brown, his wife Susan, and her son Jonathan amble out into the main hallway of the emergency wing of Starr County Hospital and make their way to the parking lot entrance where John catches a glimpse of Willito and Carmen with their baby girl. John waves to catch Willito's attention and calls him over.

Willito and Carmen turn and head toward them to greet John and his wife, who happen to be with Jonathan Manerez at the moment for some reason.

Willito walks up and extends his hand to John but looks oddly at Jonathan. "Is he in some kind of trouble, Major? Because after talking to my sister Mary, I am convinced she would be dead if it were not for this man."

John assures Willito that Jonathan is in no trouble and then quickly explains the story how that Susan is Jonathan's mother and how he just learned this truth a few moments ago.

"But that is not the reason I called you over here. I have something I want to give you."

Major John Brown, Commander of Sector D for the Texas Rangers reaches in his shirt pocket and pulls out a letter and a small black case and hands them to Willito. With a slight hesitation, Willito takes the items and opens the case first. Inside is a small round badge with a lone Texas star in the middle. Willito looks up at John.

"Really?"

John pats Willito on the shoulder. "Son, I have been a Texas Ranger for over forty years now and I know a brother when I see one. You start in two weeks. That is, if you want the job."

Willito looks over at Carmen who has her hand covering her mouth in joyful exuberance. She vigorously shakes her head *yes*. He then looks back at John and says, "Major, that is a HELL TO THE YES." Willito and Carmen say their thanks and goodbyes and head over to the room where the rest of their family is visiting with Captain Williams. The Browns, accompanied by Jonathan, walk to his car to find a quiet place to talk.

When Willito and Carmen get to Tommy's room, it's like a wall-to-wall party in there but they somehow manage to squeeze in. Tommy is lying on the bed with his shoulder bandaged up. He's obviously on some type of powerful pain reliever because he is ranting about what a hot momma he met in Mexico City and that he wants to go visit her as soon as possible. Jacob is standing in front of the bed with his mom, dad, wife, and Danielle. He also has Roberto content in his arms who, earlier in the evening, ran up to and jumped into his dad's arms as soon as he laid eyes on him, and there he remains still clinging to Dad. Isabella stands next to her husband, the elder Roberto, and their sons. Chris is next to Danielle, and Captain Phillips and Barbara are right next to them. Alex Maelstrom, Chuck Yeager, and John Bliss stand close to Jacob.

Jacob thinks that Tommy is about to get a little too uncomfortably graphic and clears his throat loudly to interrupt him. "I am sorry, sir, but I know how you get when you have a few too many and right now you are pretty full of morphine. There are some women and children present so we better save that story for later. But," he quickly segues, "I want to say something to all of you."

Everyone quiets down and Jacob continues. "Everyone in this room has had a great deal to do with my family's freedom. For that, I can never thank you enough. Just so you know, I think of all of you as my dearest friends and family. I am going home with my family to resume my life, but I just want to throw this out there. Let's never do anything like this again."

Cheers and applause erupt and the room is filled with laughter and mirth.

Jacob raises his hand. "But if any of you, and I mean any of you, want to join the Edwards family for Christmas this year, we'll throw a party like none you have never seen."

Chapter Twelve

Epilogue

Manheim, Pennsylvania, A Few Days Later

After returning to Manheim, Pennsylvania, the Edwards are right back at work, except for Jim. He's at home getting things back in order. Linda finds it a little upsetting that he closed up her beautiful home and practically abandoned it to live in his little cottage while she was "dead." So Jim's priority is to get it back into shape and enjoy some time with her at home.

Jim, however, manages to get away from home for the Manheim Auto Auction Friday sale, the first one together again as a family with Jacob and Danielle. He couldn't be more pleased. The trio excitedly enters the facility through the glass doors that lead into auction lane number one. They are greeted by hundreds of other wholesalers, auction employees, and Manheim recon workers who all cheer for a good five minutes before the sale starts.

Within a few days, Vice President Harry Rogers, former Commandant of the Coast Guard, makes a personal visit to Edwards Auto to see Jacob. Much to everyone's astonishment, he presents a full and complete pardon granted by the president of the United States of America to Jacob, absolving him of anything to do with Cozumel once and for all. Along with the pardon, Harry shows Jacob that he received a retrograde promotion to the rank of full captain, and the record shows him as Captain Jacob

Edwards, U.S. Coast Guard Retired, instead of a commander. Jim breaks into tears over the incredible news.

Jonathan and Marnia marry within six weeks of the Falcon Lake incident. The wedding is huge and held in South Texas. Reverend Roberto Garcia presides as the officiating clergy. Jacob Edwards acts as the father of the bride and gives Marnia's hand into Jonathan's.

Jonathan's mother surprises him with proof that he was born in the United States, and not Mexico, with a birth certificate signed by an OBGYN in Los Angeles, California. The name on the birth certificate reads: *Jonathan Robert Carmichael*, his mother's maiden name. Although he is now penniless in relation to his father, Jonathan finds out that his maternal grandparents set up a trust fund for him when he was born and it is now worth almost two million dollars. As a U.S. citizen with his newly married wife, he and Marnia decide to settle down in America and not Mexico. She gives up command of the Mexican Anti-Cartel Task Force to the newly promoted Major Amilio Rohos.

Jacob and Danielle work through all the details of the Harrington Enterprises and Sebastion Auto Sales holdings that she legally inherited through Boris's fiasco. They find there is nothing really left of it but Yuri's legitimate wholesaling and trucking operation. So they sell the whole thing to Jonathan and Marnia for a little over one million dollars. It's a low price, but sort of an additional wedding gift, and besides, they are ecstatic about working with Jonathan in the same business. Marnia, however, becomes a private law enforcement consultant working for Deputy Director Chuck Yeager of the FBI and also consulting with Captain Tommy Williams when he calls in for different "top secret" requests.

Danielle takes the money from the sale and donates it to the dance academy she used to teach in South Texas. Business at

Edwards Auto is booming with all the attention and excitement of having the Edwards family back together and many of their old contacts and clients return to them as their primary source for auto work. Jim, however, decides that his main priority in life from now on is Linda, his wife, so he tells Jacob that he'll be around, but he's taking a back seat in the business so he can focus on enjoying his life with her.

Captain Larry Phillips and Barbara announce their engagement a few weeks after Jonathan and Marnia's marriage. It will be another beautiful wedding and reunion in South Texas. Everyone is happy for them and glad they found each other.

Jonathan's mother and stepfather, Major and Mrs. John Brown, retire later that year and buy a home in Lancaster, Pennsylvania where they decide to live six months out of the year to be close to Jonathan and Marnia and the Edwards. John can never see himself leaving Texas completely but does not mind being away during those scorching hot South Texas summer months.

Maximillian Manerez is sentenced to death by a court in Texas but appeals the sentence and engages in a drawn out legal process. Natasha and Peter are never heard from again after the United States Federal government arrests them and takes them into custody.

Reverend Roberto and Isabella Garcia find themselves very busy these days. Their home Bible Fellowship is so huge that Roberto has to ask his ministry leadership for their help with his church group in providing some leadership who can help him to start new home fellowships and Bible studies in his area. The impact of his Bible work and the fame of his law enforcement sons and their affiliation with the Edwards family spreads throughout Starr County, Texas.

The dock at Roberto's restaurant, Jacob's Ladder, is expanded and several cruise lines make it a regular stop during their tours.

Jacob's Ladder, already a National Landmark, is so incredibly popular that people come from miles around to visit and learn about the Hero of Cozumel and how that led to The Cartel Crusher. Roberto and his family enjoy almost a celebrity status because of the place and it opens doors for Roberto to preach the Word as he tells the story of how God worked to protect his family. Roberto never convinces Jacob to visit the place, but anyone who visits Jacobs's office at Edwards Auto will see a picture of it hanging on the wall behind his desk.

Christmas that year is the biggest the Edwards family has ever hosted or seen. Everybody comes. Linda and Mary Edwards worked tirelessly for weeks to make sure all their guests are housed and taken care of. Tommy brings Rosemary Sargent up from Mexico City to enjoy the festivities. They stay in a nice hotel in Hershey nearby.

Danielle, meanwhile, continues to go down to South Texas once or twice a month to handle Edwards Auto business where she spends time with newly promoted Lieutenant Commander Chris Rottanelli. She visits the dance studio and enjoys fellowships with Grandpa Roberto while she is there. Chris helps Roberto with responsibilities in the fellowship to make it easier on him.

One Year after the Manerez Hacienda
Falcon Lake Incident

Jacob Edwards, the president of Edwards Auto, eagerly talks to his newly hired trucking and diesel mechanic manager. He picks up his phone and dials the extension for his vice president's office. "Danielle, can you come in here? I want you to meet our new trucking and diesel mechanic manager."

Danielle is a bit flustered. She just arrived in her office and already has been confronted with several phone calls and urgent matters that need to be handled, and now she gets this call to meet the new trucking manager. "Be right there."

In addition to all the work, she is a little anxious because today is the day that Chris told her he would be deciding whether to stay on active duty or not. Every time the phone rings, chills go up and down her spine in anticipation of the news. She rushes down the hall and heads to Dad's office. She opens the door and steps in.

"Good morning, Daddy. I'm here. Is this our new trucking manager?" She is focused on her dad as she nods toward the man who is seated with his back toward her in front of and facing Jacob's desk.

The man stands up and whirls around. Danielle gasps and her heart goes into her throat at the sight of Lieutenant Commander Chris Rottanelli.

"Chris, you didn't tell me you were coming. Are you—" She turns her head to her father with a fierce look on her face. "Why didn't you tell me he was in line for this job?" She huffs. "And you, *Mister* Rottanelli, now, I presume, why didn't you call me first and give me a heads up?"

Chris laughs and says, "Yes, Danielle, I separated from the Coast Guard and now you're my boss and I have something very important I want to ask you about something I want to do here at Edwards Auto, but I had to talk it over with your dad first."

"And what would that be, *Mister* Rottanelli?"

Right on time the doors that enter Jacob's office, one from the hall and one from Mary's adjacent office, open up to reveal the entire family and more are there—Roberto and Isabella, Mom with little Roberto who runs over and grabs Jacob's hand, Jim, Linda, Jonathan and Marnia, and even Chris's parents.

Still in utter shock at the sudden appearance of her entire family and Chris's parents, she spins toward Chris for an explanation only to see that he has dropped to one knee and is presenting to her a little black box, which he opens as soon as she looks at him. He shows her the most beautiful diamond ring she has ever seen and looks into her dazzling eyes and says, "Danielle Isabella Edwards, will you marry me?"

She is so blown away at the complete surprise and suddenness of everything and the intense emotions she is feeling in her body that she just barely manages to smile and nod her head yes. Chris takes her hand and places the engagement ring on her finger holding it there as he looks deeply into her eyes.

They are locked in this beautiful gaze that speaks more than any words could ever tell when suddenly little Roberto breaks away from his father's hand and darts over to where Chris kneels in front of Danielle. He places his hand on top of theirs and says, "I like Chris. He's going to be my brother now."

Everyone laughs and rejoices in gladness as Jacob says to Chris, "Well kid, you did it. With Little Roberto's approval you now have the whole family backing you up."

The End

CPSIA information can be obtained
at www.ICGtesting.com
Printed in the USA
BVHW070921290719
554567BV00012B/549/P

9 780578 546223